Praise for

"Clever, scary, and wickedly funny. I inhaled Bora Chung's book of ghost stories and then slept with the light on!" —**Avni Doshi, author *Burnt Sugar***

"Electrifying. A feast of a book. Strange, hypnotic, and audacious." —**Irenosen Okojie, author of *Speak Gigantular***

"Bora Chung's *Cursed Bunny* mines those places where what we fear is true and what is true meet and separate and re-meet. The resulting stories are indelible. Haunting, funny, gross, terrifying—and yet when we reach the end, we just want more." —**Alexander Chee, author of *How to Write an Autobiographical Novel***

"If you were the kind of child who was enthralled by *Scary Stories to Read in the Dark*, Bora Chung writes for you. Like the work of Carmen Maria Machado and Aoko Matsuda, Chung's stories are so wonderfully, blisteringly strange and powerful that it's almost impossible to put *Cursed Bunny* down. In short, this collection may, in fact, be a cursed object in the best possible way." —**Kelly Link, bestselling author of *Get in Trouble***

"Anton Hur's nimble translation manages to capture the tricky magic of Chung's voice—its wry humor and overarching coolness broken by sudden, thrilling dips into passages of vivid description. Even as Chung presents a catalog of grotesqueries that range from unsettling to seared-into-the-brain disturbing, her

power is in restraint. She and Hur always keep the reader at a slight distance in order for the more chilling twists to land with maximum impact, allowing us to walk ourselves into the trap."
—**Violet Kupersmith**, *The New York Times Book Review*

"[These] stories are beyond imagination: breathtaking, wild, crazy, the most original fiction I have ever encountered. . . . each more astounding than the last."
—**Louisa Ermelino**, *Publishers Weekly*

"Sharp, wildly inventive, and slightly demented (in the most enjoyable way, of course) . . . All we can say is buckle in, because when these stories take their horrific turn there's no setting them down." —***Chicago Review of Books***

"Nothing concentrates the mind like Chung's terrors, which will shrivel you to a bouillon cube of your most primal instincts." —**Rhoda Feng**, *Vulture*

"Chung builds out her stories with imagination, absurdity and a dry sense of humor, all applied with X-Acto knife precision, but what stands out about her fantastical tales is not how different they are from one another so much as how much remains the same."
—**Alexandra Kleeman**, *The New York Times Book Review*

"Disturbing, chilling, wrenching, and absolute genius. I wanted Chung to write a story about a reader getting a deep look inside her fantastic swirling mind. I had to take breaks and gulps of air before plunging back into each story. Magnetic, eerie, immensely important."
—**Frances Cha**, author of *If I Had Your Face*

"Cool, brilliantly demented K-horror—just the way I like it!" —**Ed Park, author of *Personal Days***

"Imagining a utopia and mourning when it falls short are the first steps toward creating a better world. A big job for fiction; Chung's up to the task. The imagined worlds here may not be utopian—but the reading experience is." —***Kirkus Reviews*, starred review**

"This Korean debut collection is a stunner. The stories included are absurdly unique, delightfully monstrous, horrifically insightful and chillingly satisfying."
—***Ms.* magazine**

"If you want a spooky set of stories that will crawl under your skin and burrow into your marrow and stay there forever, Chung's collection is a freaky, unforgettable outing. There's a folkloric quality to this collection, like these are urban legends that have finally been put to paper." —***Wired* magazine**

"Like a family in a home, fantastic stories gather together in this book. The stories not only take their revenge, but also love you, and comfort you. You'll end up completely endeared to this fascinating collection!"
—**Kyung-Sook Shin, *New York Times* bestselling author of *Please Look After Mom* and *Violets***

"The strange and everyday are melded in these startling and original tales . . . *Cursed Bunny* is [Chung's] first book to be translated into English, and hopefully not the last." —**Connie Biewald, *San Francisco Chronicle***

"This is another fantastic collection . . . that combines big topics such as technology, human absurdity, and mortality. And [Chung] does it in the most amazing ways." —*Book Riot*

"Bora Chung's stories glisten at the border of our weird world, and all our other weird worlds. A truly sublime book." —**Samantha Hunt, bestselling author of** *The Seas* **and** *The Unwritten Book*

"Unexpected, funny, thrillingly original. These stories will stick with me." —**Ainslie Hogarth, author of the** *New York Times* **Best Book of the Year** *Motherthing*, **and** *Normal Women*

"A collection of exquisitely crafted, spooky and unnerving tales that haunted me long after reading. Each story is a macabre gem, shot through with visceral horror, wry humor, and subtly profound insights on human nature. These stories convey how the traumas and transgressions of the past, individual and collective, and erupt into the present, distorting and eroding our perception of reality. Bora Chung is an amazingly inventive and daring writer. I will revisit these stories whenever I need a reminder of how fresh and vital prose can be." —**Kate Folk, author of** *Out There*

"Such a fun collection of short stories infused with speculative tendencies, Slavic literary traditions, and extremely relatable pandemic-era fears."
—**Jennifer Croft,** *Los Angeles Daily News*

"Through the prism of her singular imagination, Chung looks sharply at the ways the world we've made doesn't suit us. . . . These are stories to sit with, to read one at a time and savor." —*Esquire*

"A gut-punch reminder of our own humanity or lack thereof. It urges readers not only to be kinder, but also to be wide-eyed about the technological world around them. This is a book to slip into your friend's hand with a knowing nod and a wordless 'trust me' implied."
—*Scientific American*

"Hur returns as Chung's brilliant Korean-to-English cipher for eight more enigmatically irresistible stories. . . . Chung's electrifying author's note offers provenance for many of her stories and an empathic invitation to progress 'toward a better world for both you and me.'"
—*Booklist*, starred review

"Bora Chung has proven once again that she is an undeniable maestro of the uncanny, grotesque, and posthuman. Only a consummate speculative allegorist could write a collection that functions as so haunting a mirror of our modern world, reminding us all the while that the politely deranged cannibals and lovesick AIs and beleaguered alien wives we see reflected in that mirror are really just versions of ourselves."
—Rafael Frumkin, author of *Confidence* and *The Comedown*

"If you are looking for stories that are reminiscent of 'Black Mirror' or that peek into the unknown, surrounding, burgeoning AI and make one generally question what it means to be human, then *Your Utopia* is for you." —Bookreporter.com

"Fables of frightening moral clarity told in calm, bell-like prose, *Cursed Bunny* aims to unsettle. It's as assured and brilliant as a nightmare. With an unflinching gaze and a sly humor, Chung has built a world both unfamiliar and eerily familiar, whose truths echo into our own. The indelible work of a master." —**Shruti Swamy, author of** *The Archer* **and** *A House Is a Body*

"Uncanny atmospheres and heartfelt human insights strike an unlikely balance . . . Chung lingers tenderly with the emotional depths of her stories, which arise almost unexpectedly as her characters navigate surreal, speculative, and often mundanely horrifying horizons." —*Shelf Awareness*

"Chung has crafted another weird and surprising story collection . . . Central to the collection is an exploration of loneliness and isolation, but Chung is far too complex a writer to simply blame technology for these shortcomings. . . . She plays with our expectations of the future, experiments with the possibilities of what could be, and sprinkles in elements from other genres to keep the stories fresh." —*Chicago Review of Books*

"Whether borrowing from fable, folktale, speculative fiction, science fiction, or horror, Chung's stories corkscrew toward devastating conclusions—bleak, yes, but also wise and honest about the nightmares of contemporary life. Don't read this book while eating—but don't skip these unflinching, intelligent stories, either." —*Kirkus Reviews,* starred review

"Chung debuts with a well-crafted and horrifying collection of dark fairy tales, stark revenge fables, and disturbing body horror. Clever plot twists and sparkling prose abound. Chung's work is captivating and terrifying." —*Publishers Weekly*

"[A] get-under-your-skin collection" —*LitHub*

"This short story collection is like a car crash you can't look away from: grotesque in the best way . . . Each story is fantastically unique, and unlike anything I've ever read before." —Kirby Beaton, *BuzzFeed*'s Best December Books of 2022

"Bora Chung's stories succeed at being deeply visceral experiences that do what the best fairy tales do: convey the unspeakable in a way that is nevertheless collectively understood . . . perfect for fans of Bong Joon-ho's films or Helen Oyeyemi's fiction."
—Alice Martin, *Shelf Awareness*

MIDNIGHT TIMETABLE

Also by Bora Chung

Your Utopia

Cursed Bunny: Stories

MIDNIGHT TIMETABLE

A NOVEL IN GHOST STORIES

BY BORA CHUNG

Translated by Anton Hur

ALGONQUIN BOOKS OF CHAPEL HILL
LITTLE, BROWN AND COMPANY

The characters and events in this book are fictitious.
Any similarity to real persons, living or dead, is coincidental
and not intended by the author.

Copyright © 2025 by Bora Chung
Translation © 2025 by Anton Hur

Hachette Book Group supports the right to free expression and the value of copyright. The purpose of copyright is to encourage writers and artists to produce the creative works that enrich our culture.

The scanning, uploading, and distribution of this book without permission is a theft of the author's intellectual property. If you would like permission to use material from the book (other than for review purposes), please contact permissions@hbgusa.com. Thank you for your support of the author's rights.

Algonquin Books of Chapel Hill / Little, Brown and Company
Hachette Book Group
1290 Avenue of the Americas, New York, NY 10104
algonquinbooks.com

First Edition: September 2025

Algonquin Books of Chapel Hill is an imprint of Little, Brown and Company, a division of Hachette Book Group, Inc. The Algonquin Books name and logo are trademarks of Hachette Book Group, Inc.

The publisher is not responsible for websites (or their content) that are not owned by the publisher.

The Hachette Speakers Bureau provides a wide range of authors for speaking events. To find out more, go to hachettespeakersbureau.com or email hachettespeakers@hbgusa.com.

Little, Brown and Company books may be purchased in bulk for business, educational, or promotional use. For information, please contact your local bookseller or the Hachette Book Group Special Markets Department at special.markets@hbgusa.com.

ISBN 978-1-64375-663-9 (hardcover)

ISBN 978-1-64375-666-0 (ebook)

LCCN 2025938839

Printing 1, 2025

LSC-C

Printed in the United States of America

Table of Contents

You Can't Come in Here   1

Handkerchief   35

Cursed Sheep   73

Silence of the Sheep   99

Blue Bird   131

Why Does the Cat   147

Sunning Day   173

Afterword: On the Joys of Ghost Stories   183

MIDNIGHT TIMETABLE

You Can't Come in Here

"You can't come in here."

That's what the man who stood behind the parking lot door said to Sook when she opened it.

The man looked utterly nondescript. A nondescript build. A nondescript dark suit. A voice and manner of speaking that was all very nondescript. The kind of person she would've immediately forgotten if she'd passed him on the street. But she hadn't passed him on the street, she'd been stopped by him at the Institute's basement-level parking lot.

"It's not that he had no characteristics whatsoever. You could say his being exceedingly nondescript was a characteristic."

Sook said this much later on. She also mentioned that the overhead lights in the parking lot happened to hit the man's ID tag at just the right angle, so the glare obscured the text. Was *that* a characteristic?

Sook did not, at the time, think too deeply about the nondescript nature of the man. That's just the nature of the nondescript, you see.

Instead, she asked him, "Why can't I come in? Is something going on?"

Sook had been working at the Institute for some time now. She always came down the stairs to the underground parking lot after the evening's work and took her car home. The parking lot exit was a little creepy to begin with, but this was the first time someone had actively stopped her from going on her way. It unsettled her and made her nervous.

"You have to go up a floor," said the mysterious man in an even tone, not answering Sook's question.

"But I need to get to my car."

Sook had assumed the man, who was obviously some employee or other, hadn't realized she drove to work. He must've thought she'd meant to leave by the ground-floor entrance of the Institute building. But that exit led to the empty fields that surrounded the center, and there was no public transportation nearby. Sook hardly lived within walking distance from work; there was no way she could go home without her car, which was currently parked in the basement level.

"You have to go up a floor," the man repeated.

Sook took a moment to think about it and decided

to give up, as the man clearly was not concerned with giving her an explanation. No one bothered to explain things to "the cleaning lady." Sook knew this all too well from years of experience, not just as a "cleaning lady" but as a "lady" in general. She let go of the doorknob and went back up the stairs. Her plan was to go up a floor, walk to the other end of the building, and take the elevator down the other side.

As she made her way up, the parking lot door she had left open behind her closed on its own. She was on the second step when it slammed shut, and the sound echoed through the stairwell and sent an involuntary shiver down her spine. Sook quickly made her way up the stairs and opened the door to the lobby.

Instead, she came out into the parking lot.

Her hand still on the doorknob, she stared disbelievingly around her. Here was her car, the old white hunk of junk she had come to work in that morning.

But the research center building only had one basement level. She turned around. Behind her was the same stairwell she had walked up and down for the past nine years. Her movement retriggered the light sensors and they blinked on. Sook stared hard behind her into the stairwell.

There were no stairs going down.

This was the story a sunbae at the center told me when I asked her if she had heard anything strange from the people on the night watch shift. I had just started to work at the Institute, and she was in charge of showing me the ropes, mostly because her shift ended as mine started. I would come up to the employees' lounge and find her there, sitting in front of a steaming mug of tea, always in the same seat at the big table.

"Sook unni had worked here the longest," my sunbae said. "She told me that story herself right after she quit."

"She quit because of that?"

"No. She quit because of her kids."

A very ordinary reason. Sook had raised three children alone. Her third child had had some kind of medical condition since birth. The life insurance payout after her husband's car accident had been depleted fairly rapidly, with all the third child's hospital fees, examinations, and medicine, as well as the added inconvenience of the four surviving family members requiring constant nourishment and a roof over their heads. Sook had to work at a restaurant by day and took on watch duties at the Institute by night. She managed to send her first and second child to good universities and to save enough money for her third child's operation. Sook quit the Institute when she moved to a city that had those good universities and hospital.

"She said her life's dream was to sleep under the same roof with her kids every night," said my sunbae.

"Good for her," I said. This Sook was not someone I knew personally, but it moved me to think of a parent who had raised three children alone finally achieving her life's dream.

"I'm sure that unni had other things happen to her that she didn't tell me about," said my sunbae. "Because I saw that flashy thing myself."

"*You* saw something?" I said, but I immediately regretted my faux pas. "I'm sorry."

My sunbae grinned. "Believe me, I was also very surprised that I did. I didn't know what it meant to actually see something until that moment."

What my sunbae had seen was a whitish blur. A blur that would grow more intense or fainter and larger and smaller and then disappear.

"I saw it going up the stairs."

"So what did you do?" I was hanging onto her every word.

"I just turned around and went back down." She might as well have shrugged. "What else could I do?"

I was a little disappointed. But my sunbae became serious.

"You can't react when that happens to you. Don't try to touch it or anything. Never say things like, 'Is anyone there?' The moment you acknowledge its existence, it'll come into creation right inside your mind and grow. You'll be drawn in, then consumed."

"How do you know that?" I exclaimed. "Do

you have a special third eye because you're blind, or something?"

My sunbae grinned again. I was mortified and wanted to sink into the floor, right through to the Institute's "nonexistent" second basement. "I'm so sorry, that's not—"

"I think I can work at the Institute precisely because I can't see," she mused. "Some sighted people don't last for more than three days here. They make up stuff that doesn't exist, they see things and hear things. And those things become real and haunt them. When they never existed in the first place."

My sunbae went back to her story about the "flashy" thing. She was going up the steps when that large blob appeared before her. Having been blind since birth, my sunbae had never seen an object, any object, in her life. She couldn't immediately comprehend that she was seeing for the first time. It was surprising, but not painful or dreadful at first, which was why she took a moment to consider it before dismissing it for the time being. She could always think more about this experience when she got back to her room to sleep.

Having decided this, she was going up the staircase when she suddenly lost count of the steps. Eight steps from the bottom, and then the landing, and then eight more steps in the next flight. But how many steps left from the top? Had she gone up four just now? Five?

As she pondered this, the whitish object she was seeing became larger, the white more intense. This was shocking to experience for the first time. And terrifying.

My sunbae did not have her white cane with her. After she had gotten used to the internal layout of the Institute, or the layout of the parts we were allowed to go into at least, she rarely brought her cane with her. This was the first time she had ever regretted leaving her room without her cane.

She began to walk backward. Never had she walked down a flight of steps backward before. She had to bend over and touch the stairs as she almost crawled down. There was no one else in the building and no one else would be in the building until the morning. My sunbae was alone. She did not even carry her phone with her on night watch rounds. If she fell down these stairs, that would be the end of her.

She had gone down two or three steps when she immediately became confused. Her hands had touched two stairs, but her feet felt like they'd gone down three. Or had she gone down three with her feet but only counted two with her hands? The blob that had shrunken was becoming larger and whiter again.

My sunbae gave up counting steps. She went down the stairs as quickly as possible.

Her feet touched the landing. Her knees bumped up on flat ground. So did her hands. My sunbae touched her knees and feet. She made sure that her feet and hands were done with being on different stairs and that she was safe on solid ground. She felt around for the wall to support her so she could get up.

Her hand touched something, not something solid. A person's hand. The hand was warm and soft—and pale, she somehow knew—and had thin fingers with a firm grip that enclosed my sunbae's hand. My sunbae whipped her hand away, but before she could scream, the hand was no longer there. When she felt around her once more, she could only feel the hard wall.

"And then what happened?" I could hardly breathe at that point.

"I went back upstairs and went to sleep," she said simply.

I was disappointed. "That's it?"

My sunbae told me that she had stood for a while, leaning on the wall. Then, having calmed down, she began to go up the steps. Knowing that she would only get confused again if she used her hands to touch the steps, she climbed them upright while she felt along the wall, as she usually did.

One, two, three, four, five, six, seven.

Before the last, eighth step, my sunbae hesitated. She feared that a warm hand would grab hers again, or a whitish, large blob would appear before her unseeing eyes.

Right next to her ear, someone whispered:

—*Go up a step.*

My sunbae tore up the steps with all her might. She ran down a corridor in a panic until she crashed against a wall. She had to stop then. She felt around that wall and found the door to her dorm room. She ran inside, slammed the door shut, and threw herself on the bed.

My sunbae murmured, "But when I went back outside later and touched the wall, there was nothing there. It was just the hard wall."

I didn't understand. "What do you mean? All walls are hard. Or did you feel some kind of padded wall?" The Institute was a research center, not a psychiatric hospital. There were no padded walls here. At least, all the walls I had seen in the building were regular.

My sunbae hesitated before saying, "When I slammed into it, it was soft."

We were silent for a moment.

"Then . . . he actually exists."

"Who exists?" asked my sunbae. She knew what I was talking about but was insisting I spell it out.

"You didn't make up someone that doesn't exist, you saw him and heard his voice and . . . collided into him."

"But I must never admit that," she said quietly. "I have to pretend that he's not there, pretend I don't know. That's the only way we can keep working here."

That's when my sunbae told me about the other person who had worked here after the unni had quit.

Chan was a queer man who was being treated for hallucinations. These were the two facts about him that Chan told my sunbae on his first day of work. Chan had learned he was queer at a very young age. His family, meanwhile, were religious fanatics. The religion they zealously adhered to had strict rules governing the manner in which people should exist, and they liked to perpetuate discrimination and hate according to these arbitrary tenets. Chan, torn between the way he was born and the religious tenets that condemned him, discussed his dilemma with a leader of his religion. This leader violated every ethical and legal principle in the books by swiftly conveying the contents of this discussion to Chan's parents. Chan's parents, on the leader's recommendation, used their authority over this minor to force their child to go to "ex-gay" conditioning. But sexual orientation not being a disease, and a person becoming conditioned to "ex" their sexuality also not being a feasible proposition, the treatment served only to torture him rather than to change him.

Chan experienced all sorts of violence and violations of human rights in the conditioning facility. He sustained a permanent physical injury and post-traumatic stress syndrome on top of that. But these conditions exempted him from the military, and he became fairly adept at ignoring the hallucinations, which is why Chan didn't consider it to be an altogether bad thing.

"But that is absolutely an altogether bad thing," my sunbae had said to him. "Have you thought of suing them or reporting them?"

"I don't want to even think about them or have to be involved with them again in any way," Chan replied.

My sunbae understood. So she simply explained to him what the job involved.

"Please turn your phone off during work, and don't carry it around with you if possible. If there's an accident or a situation you really can't handle, use one of the red emergency phones on the walls."

Chan took his phone out of his pocket and switched it off. As he put the phone back in his pocket, he asked, "Are you guys worried about . . . confidential research being leaked?"

"No. It's just that ghosts like communication devices."

Chan didn't answer. My sunbae, who was unable to see his expression, continued to explain.

"Even with the phones off, you might still get a call. While you're working here, and even when you're off duty, you shouldn't be answering phone calls when you're alone and in a dark place."

My sunbae had given me the same instructions when I started. She couldn't see my expression either then, but I'm sure she was enjoying my reaction regardless.

"On your rounds, you only have to check if all the room doors are locked. And if you hear a sound, don't ever look back." She had paused here. "I said, don't ever look back."

I had almost jumped out of my skin because I was looking back. My sunbae smiled.

Chan, however, had been calm when she'd told him this. "Did you think I was looking back?" he asked. "Because I wasn't."

Chan was trained in such things. There were many kinds of hallucinations, such as the seeing of things that didn't exist, or hearing voices that weren't really there, the kind of hallucinations in movies. Less commonly known hallucinations, however, included smelling nonexistent smells or feeling nonexistent textures.

The human body is our fundamental method of existing in and relating to this world we live in. Chan's body, however, used every sense it had to fool him. And it was Chan's belief that his body was his burden to endure in this life, that he had to endure this burden because he was a wrong and broken person, and there was no solution for it nor escape from it. In truth, Chan's beliefs had been forcibly conditioned in him. And whenever his despair and confusion got to be too much to bear, he sought the help of Gak.

Gak was someone who had at one time been a part of the same religion that Chan had been a part of. Gak's family had also taken an uncritical stance of the religion they followed. After Gak cut ties with his family, the religious group condemned him as a personification of evil who had no path to salvation because he had chosen the filthy life of a sinner, casting aside his own family. When Chan's family abused Chan, they sometimes compared him to Gak, saying they were of the same ilk, which was why Gak's name was seared into Chan's memory.

It was Gak who took Chan to a real psychiatric hospital. There, Chan discovered actual salvation. That there was a name for the sustained chaos he experienced and there were ways of managing it, and experts who were willing to take him seriously and help him. They offered him a sense of peace so profound that Chan could not find the words to describe it.

Gak took the time and care to explain to Chan that he was not a "failure of treatment" or a "mistake of a human being," instead using precise legal terms like assault, unlawful arrest, and unlawful use of threat to explain the abuse done to Chan and how his current symptoms were a result of such abuse. Chan listened closely to Gak and slowly began to understand what had been done to him. He was able to mourn the life he had lost to his suffering and take his first steps toward a better future where he was able to take care of himself. This job he got at a research center for haunted objects, where he would check the doors of rooms along corridors that either existed or didn't exist, according to some midnight timetable, was Chan taking his first steps toward "normality"; he was doing regular paid work that was at the same time not so overwhelming in terms of regular human interaction, which he still wasn't quite ready for.

Gak was against him taking the job. It worried him that the Institute was so secluded, and that Chan was unable to clearly explain exactly what this research center actually researched. In the midst of their ensuing argument, Gak tried to kiss Chan. Chan pushed him off and ran away. He could not admit to himself, still, that he wanted to wholly embrace Gak as he was kissing him, that Gak's unspoken confession of his affection made him deeply happy. After that, Chan did not pick up Gak's calls and did not return to see him.

At the beginning of every shift at the Institute, Chan turned off his phone and locked it in the saddle pouch of his motorcycle. Taking his flashlight, he would go up to the first floor, scan in with his ID, and slowly start his rounds. He sometimes bumped into employees who were leaving late from their own shifts and would say hello. After 8 p.m., he turned off the building's lights. If he ever bumped into the occasional employee after lights out, he never looked too closely to see if they were actual people or not. He took one step on the staircase at a time and checked to see if all the doors in all the corridors were locked, pulling at each door, until he reached the top floor where the employees' lounge was. There, he would have a cup of tea, and if he ran into my sunbae there, have a chat with her. Then, at a set time, he would leave the lounge and go down the corridors floor by floor again, carefully checking each doorknob. The round, steely doorknobs were always cold to the touch, the doors were always locked, and there were rarely any people, strange sounds, or strange smells in the dark corridors. Chan came to regard the dark corridors not with fear but as spaces of peace and order. Because those spaces were not "normal," Chan could finally be normal in contrast to them. But because the Institute was not a normal place, Chan ended up having an abnormal experience.

"It's not that there were no strange things happening whatsoever," Chan had said to my sunbae. "It's just that my life has always been full of strange things..."

A sad grin.

For example, he once heard the sound of a bird behind the closed door of a lab, the chirping and the fluttering. For several nights, when he approached that door, the bird would call out and flap. Chan wasn't sure if this sound was a hallucination or if there really was a bird trapped behind the door of that lab, so he ignored my sunbae's advice and took his phone with him one night on his rounds. When he got to the lab's door where the bird started to chirp and flap again, he recorded the sound.

At home, there was no sound on the recording. Chan concluded that the sound had been a hallucination and was reassured.

"But it wasn't a hallucination," my sunbae said to him when he mentioned the incident in passing. "There really is a bird in there. But since it's not a living bird, it's a good thing you didn't open that door."

"I see," Chan said after a long pause.

He never spoke of the bird again.

Then one day, after going down the steps to the parking lot and opening the door at the bottom, he's stopped by a stranger who blocks his way. It's morning, the end of his shift; the researchers are about to arrive for the day, and Chan had just run into the Institute's deputy director on her way in as he himself was scanning out.

"You can't come in here."

The stranger is tall, wears a dark suit, and there's a metallic something on his jacket that looks like a name tag. The ceiling light is reflecting on it so Chan can't read the name or position.

Chan doesn't answer. He has never seen this employee before. No one has ever prevented him from entering the parking lot. Such a task is normally done by security. And Chan himself is security.

So Chan ignores the stranger and tries to enter the parking lot.

"You can't come in here."

The stranger is now blocking his way, his tone still polite but firm.

Chan quickly walks past the man and into the parking lot. He then mounts his motorcycle and starts the engine. Normally, after putting on his helmet, he'd tuck his flashlight into his saddle pouch, turn on his headlights, and go slowly up the incline leading to the exit. But now Chan can't get out of there fast enough. He glimpses the stranger still standing by the stairwell, watching him. He looks taller than he had a moment ago, and his face is now completely in shadow. When Chan rides past him on his motorcycle, the stranger's name tag flashes. Chan looks straight ahead and focuses on not crashing.

He goes down a rough concrete path toward a crossroad with a traffic light. It's still dark all around him and the traffic light, as always, blinks yellow. Chan carefully looks both ways before turning left. He is engulfed in darkness save for the yellow stripe of the median line illuminated by his headlight. Chan relies on the presence of that line as he cautiously rides on.

The yellow median veers left and right as Chan follows it along the winding road.

The yellow median veers left.

The yellow median veers right.

The yellow median twists diagonally to the left. Alongside the road are signs with white lettering warning CURVE AHEAD and SLOW DOWN and DRIVE SLOWLY as well as yellow signs with black arrows pointing this way and that. Beyond them is total darkness where nothing is visible.

The yellow median veers right.

Chan begins to think, at this point, that something is amiss. The route down from the Institute and heading left at the first crossroads is supposed to lead to a downtown area after about half an hour. Even accounting for the early hour where most shops would not be open, he at least should've seen a few twenty-four-hour convenience stores with their fluorescent lights and signage, as well as the gas stations that are open at all hours. Not to mention the fact that there should be no incline on the route between the Institute and the town.

Chan slows his speed. But then, he changes his mind. If he wanted to check his path, he would have to park his motorcycle in the dark somewhere, open his saddle pouch, and take out his phone. He doesn't want to park in the complete darkness that could be the edge of a deep cliff for all he could see. The sun will surely rise in a little while. Once he can see around him, he'll be able to find his way. Which is why Chan speeds up again, following the median to wherever it may take him.

A sign flashes past overhead.

TUNNEL AHEAD, LENGTH 1,682 KM.

Before he has a chance to wonder about the strangely long length of the tunnel, he's in it.

The lights are so bright inside that Chan instantly feels reassured. He couldn't see behind or ahead of him in the darkness outside, but here in the tunnel the lights are bright and there are emergency exits and phones at set intervals. He is startled by the sound of a police car siren but soon realizes it's just a recorded sound that must be played to keep drowsy drivers awake.

Then, in the green-tinged light of the tunnel's interior, Chan wonders how a hallucination could be so vivid. There has never been a tunnel between the Institute and his home. Either the tunnel itself is a hallucination, or he has completely lost his way and is riding off to some other region. Neither prospect appeals to him.

There is a green emergency exit sign on the left. It has a green person running toward a white rectangle of light, and the number 7 is affixed above that sign, also in green. Farther down the tunnel is the sign again with the number 5. On the ceiling there's another sign indicating how much of the tunnel remains ahead:

TO EXIT: 2,835 KM.

A strange number to begin with—shouldn't it be rounded up or down? And the remainder of the tunnel is apparently longer than what the sign he'd seen before he entered had said. Either the sign—one of the signs—or this whole tunnel is a hallucination.

The thought of his not knowing where he really is and what he's doing here makes Chan more and more afraid. But there's still the possibility that he's in a real tunnel. And he can't just stop in the middle of the tunnel.

The exit. He looks carefully at the signs around him again. Just then, he happens to pass Emergency Exit 4.

4?

The number of death, according to your typical ghost stories, a thought that makes him scoff inside his helmet. In that next moment, he passes Emergency Exit 8.

He passed 7 and 5 a long time ago and there has been no Emergency Exit 6. Chan doesn't know why, but he becomes determined to take Emergency Exit 6, if it ever shows up. Maybe, if it's something that doesn't show up in a hallucination, that's the exit to the real world.

Emergency Exit 11.

TO EXIT: 65,379 KM.

Chan parks his motorcycle in the emergency lane.

When he was getting his driver's license and buying his motorcycle, to be able to take his job at the

Institute, Chan had asked his doctor to confirm many times whether he was really allowed to drive. He got his doctor's recommendation to submit to the testing authorities and successfully obtained his license, but Chan was still very careful to read and memorize all the safety regulations surrounding the operation of his motorcycle. Following these rules, Chan turns off the engine and leaves the key in the ignition as he dismounts. He looks both ways. The tunnel is completely empty. There is only the occasional drowsiness-prevention siren faintly ringing in the distance. But he cannot discount the possibility that if this is really all a hallucination, in the real world, he could be standing in the middle of a highway, or on the rooftop of some tall building, about to take a step that could end his life. Chan hesitates and looks around him one more time.

Then, he crosses the tunnel. He runs into the emergency exit.

He pushes open the door, enters a short access corridor, and pushes open the door at the end of it. He stumbles out . . . into the same tunnel. The exit number he has come out of is marked 14. Chan looks for another sign around him. The number on the sign on the ceiling has changed as well.

TO EXIT: 7,59,36,25 KM.

There is nothing more he can do. He decides to call for help.

He reaches for his phone in his pocket but only then realizes he has left his phone in the saddle bag of his motorcycle.

Great, *now* things feel more realistic, he thinks, annoyed. Well, even if he had held the phone in his hand, there is no guarantee it would connect to a place in the world outside of this hallucination, but he still misses it. Chan looks around the tunnel again. Its rainbow-colored lighting looks positively ominous.

Chan thinks.

And then he tries to shake the thought from his mind.

The thought that: even if he goes back to the motorcycle where his phone is, who else can he call for help aside from Gak? If he uses one of the emergency phones in the tunnel to call the tunnel's management or the cops, he may lose his license. If he can't ride his motorcycle, how is he going to go to work at the Institute? He can't walk there every day. Bicycle? The distance is too far, not to mention the fact that the roads are unfit for bicycles. Would he have to quit his job if his license was revoked? How is he going to live then? There aren't many places that would pay a living wage to someone with his CV. He can't ask his family for help, not that they would even accept him if he went back to them. And even if they did, Chan would have to live under everything he had escaped from. That is not a life he could endure.

Chan thinks of Gak.

But Chan had pushed Gak away, physically and otherwise. He wracks his brain for someone else, anyone, he can contact for help, but all that comes to mind is his own desperate loneliness. Chan is completely alone and isolated in this bespoke nonreality. There is no one in the world who can experience and understand this hallucination with him, no one who is rooting for him to prevail in his quest to live a normal life in normal society despite the burdens of his broken past. But Chan still wants to ask for help. He wants to cling to someone who would reach out for his hand.

Chan thinks.

He is startled by the sound of a ringing phone. Chan looks around for the source of the ringing that is splitting his ear: it's an emergency phone hanging on the wall, to his right.

This really has to be a hallucination, he thinks. There hadn't been a phone in this spot until a moment ago, he is sure of it. Which is why he's determined not to answer the phone.

But it is unbearably loud. And—perhaps because it's a hallucination—it's getting louder. It echoes and echoes in the tunnel. Chan blocks his ears.

The ringing makes the very bones of his body vibrate. He can't stand it anymore.

Chan turns and opens the exit door from where he'd come. As soon as the door shuts behind him, the ringing ceases. He sighs in relief.

Then his relief is pierced through by the sound of another ringing phone. He looks around the access corridor. There's a red emergency phone on the wall to his right again, screaming to be picked up. There had been nothing on the walls when he had passed through this corridor a moment ago.

Chan runs out the door at the other end and just barely manages to stop himself from running into the busy traffic that wasn't there before, cars running at full speed in both directions. A large truck blares its horn at him as he teeters on the edge of the road.

Chan steps back. He can't cross now.

Something cold and hard bumps into him behind him. He turns. The emergency exit has disappeared. All that's there is a hard and gray concrete wall.

The cars run past him incredibly close, at a very high speed. He tries to plaster himself to the wall.

This is absurd. Tunnel roads always have a little

shoulder for people to walk on in case of an emergency. But there is no such shoulder to be seen. Chan has no place of safety here.

The noise from the running cars, the vibrations, and the honking of horns makes him fear for his eardrums.

What do I do?, he asks himself. There must be another emergency exit.

He needs to get away from the rushing cars as quickly as possible, to be somewhere safe. He sees a sign on the ceiling of the tunnel.

CURVE AHEAD SLOW DOWN.

As he tries to parse the meaning of this particular part of his absurd hallucination, he is startled once more by the ringing of a telephone cutting through all the noise of the cars that makes the earth shake, the blare of their horns. It's coming from an emergency phone on his left. Chan, sticking his body to the wall of the tunnel, inches his way sideways to the left. He picks up.

"Hell—"

"*When would you like your coffin delivered?*"

The voice on the other end is businesslike. Chan is thrown.

"What?"

"*The crematorium is booked full until next week, I'm afraid.*"

"What? Listen, I . . ." Clinging onto what he could remember of the emergency evacuation protocol from his motorcycle safety reading, he looks around frantically for an exit sign. "I am trying to, I'm, I called because I need some help here." He remembers then that he is not the caller, but that's hardly important right now.

"*Rescue?*" The other side seems perplexed. "*Aren't you about to be deceased?*"

"What?"

The other side ignores this and asks, "*Would you like us to deliver your shroud along with your coffin?*"

This is a hallucination. Chan breathes deeply and repeats it to himself in his mind. "This is only a hallucination."

There were a few times when he tried to kill himself. There was a long period where he had tried to deny his very existence, where he thought it would be better to just wipe himself from the face of the earth.

But now, in this moment, he wants to live.

He realized later on that what he had felt all his life was not a desire to die. It was a desire to escape the violence and abuse against him, and it was his denial of who he was and what he could become that had trapped him in this abuse. It was only recently where he had realized that death was not the only escape from that trap. It has tortured him to think of how late this realization was in coming. But as long as one is alive, he'll soon know, there is no such thing as being too late.

For now, however, he only has an inkling as to this truth, and an inkling is enough. Because what gives him the strength to fight is the fact that the person who gave him that inkling, the most important person in his life, is still somewhere outside this tunnel.

Chan speaks clearly and calmly to the person on the other end, enunciating each word as concisely as possible.

"I have no plans to be 'deceased.'"

"*Oh?*" The other side seems unfazed.

Chan's resolve hardens. "And I will not be purchasing a coffin or a shroud."

"*Ah, I see.*"

"I'm inside a tunnel," Chan says quietly. "Come rescue me. Send a hearse if you must, whatever you've got that has wheels. And if you don't rescue me, I'll walk out of here myself."

Before the other side can answer, Chan hangs up.

When he turns away from the phone, he finds the tunnel as empty as when he had first entered it. Chan begins to walk across the tunnel to where his motorcycle is parked.

"You can't come in here."

It's the tall man with the dark suit. He really is quite tall, his face in shadow. The metallic name tag flashes in Chan's eyes. He flinches.

"You can't come in here," the man repeats as Chan tries to walk past him.

"You're just a hallucination," murmurs Chan as he tries not to look him in the eye. "And I am getting out of here."

He takes a step forward. The man blocks his way. Chan decides he needs to walk through this hallucination, so he throws his whole body against the man's torso. The dark suit covers his face . . .

Chan woke to the sound of the EMS worker's voice. The sky ahead was dark. The same shade, he thought, as the suit the mysterious man had been wearing. Acrid-smelling smoke swirled around him.

". . . There was a fire in the tunnel," the EMS worker was explaining. "We're going to take you to a hospital."

Motorcycle, cell phone, Chan tried to say to the EMS worker. But an oxygen mask was being affixed over his nose and mouth and he couldn't speak. Chan's gurney was put on an ambulance and taken to the hospital.

"And that's why he quit?" I asked.

"No. After he was discharged, he continued to work here for a long time. He only quit when he and his lover decided to move to a different region."

"His lover?"

My sunbae told me the rest of the story.

Chan had been discovered in a tunnel in the opposite direction of his home, a tunnel headed for another city. There had been an accident in there and a subsequent fire. Chan had been one of the many people who had followed proper procedure by getting on an emergency phone and calling the authorities for help. He did not, however, seem to be able to explain how he got so far in the wrong direction or why he made a wrong turn in the first place. He said it was probably because of fatigue from working all night and he had become confused in the dark. There were technically no lies in this story, and the police found his explanation satisfactory.

During the two days he was in the hospital, Chan thought about the question he was asked on the emergency phone. *Aren't you about to be deceased?* About the desperate moment he wanted to reach out to someone for help, how his desperation and will to live had focused on a single person. If it had really been the end—and this was as close to that as he would ever get before the real thing—who was it that he wanted to say goodbye to the most? Who would even care to see him one last time? When he was discharged and got his phone and flashlight back after giving his statement to the police, Chan thought long and hard before calling Gak.

Gak picked up on the first ring.

"I'm so glad," I said. I even thought it was romantic. Not that what Chan went through was romantic, at all. But to have gone through hell and found someone whom you thought you'd lost, someone with whom you could weather the storms together . . . that, in all honesty, was romantic. I joked, "I guess everyone who works here ends up quitting for happy reasons?"

"Not always," said my sunbae, her expression serious. "I'll tell you that story some other time."

I was a little disappointed. My sunbae used her right index and middle fingers to feel the braille watch on her left wrist. "I think it's time for your rounds."

"All right." We got up. We left the employees' lounge. We closed the door. My sunbae went down the left side, feeling the wall as she went toward her room. I switched on my flashlight and headed down the right.

As I slowly came down the stairs, I thought about what I had neglected to tell my sunbae. It had happened a week after I had begun to work here. I'd come out of the lounge, switched on my flashlight, and went right down the dark corridor. I was halfway up the steps when a man wearing a dark suit blocked me from going forward.

"You can't come in here."

The man in the dark suit was completely nondescript. The man in Chan's story, as relayed by my sunbae, was supposed to be very tall. But this man seemed closer to the one Sook had seen. Neither his height, voice, speech, nor face had any memorable characteristics. I tilted my flashlight upward. The nondescript man's nondescript suit had a nondescript name tag on it, which caught my eye.

"Ah," I said. "Got it."

I bowed, turned, and went down the stairs. Since then, I've been especially careful when I've just come out of the employees' lounge. I don't go up the staircase at the end of the corridor, for the sole reason that the employees' lounge is on the top floor of the Institute. Instead, I turn left or right.

As I mentioned, the man I'd bumped into then, one week into my new job, had a name tag on his chest. When I shone my flashlight at it, I saw no name on it or any other designation other than the words EXECUTIVE DIRECTOR. Which was why I turned around and went back down the stairs as I was told.

At the bottom, when I looked back, the nondescript man in the dark suit still stood there in the middle of the staircase that didn't exist, looking down at me. Well, his face was obscured by shadow, so I can't be sure if he really was *looking* at me. I'm just saying I had that feeling, that's all. When I looked back, the nondescript man smiled a small, nondescript smile. At least, I think he did. It's just a feeling.

Don't ask me what the nondescript man's nondescript face looked like. I don't remember it at all.

Slowly trying the handle of each door down the right-hand-side corridor, I wondered if I should tell my sunbae the fact that the extraordinary man in the nondescript suit was the executive director of the research center. It's good to know that if I ever happen to stumble into a place I shouldn't be entering, the executive director will appear and block me. A little odd in terms of safety measures, but one very appropriate for this particular institution.

Handkerchief

"**D**o you like scary stories?"

It was my first night on the job. I nodded. The following is the first story my sunbae ever told me.

The departed had three daughters and two sons. Which was fairly common in those times. Everyone had several siblings, the more children the merrier, and many couples tried several times until they gave birth to a son.

The departed had especially loved her second son. This was not so common. Normally, parents of that era loved their eldest son the best and depended on him the most, but the departed only loved her younger son, and it was the deepest and most all-consuming love of her life. Even after her children grew up and graduated their schools and left home and created their own families, the departed's love for her younger son never changed. If anything, it burned brighter. This younger son, until his mother died, never once held a proper job or did a day's work in his life. Despite this, he wore expensive suits and shoes, drove a big, fancy car, and spent his days in resorts and ski lodges and famous beaches and hotels around the world. The money he spent on this lifestyle was provided by his mother. From his childhood to the time of this story, by which he had become a white-haired old man, he took it for granted that not only his nice houses and cars but also his every cigarette or cup of coffee should be provided by his mother.

In contrast, the mother nagged her eldest son for money as soon as he graduated college and got a job. This eldest son, thinking of his sick father and young sisters, worked very hard to make as much money as his mother wanted from him.

The eldest son also had an innocent and perhaps desperate hope that if he fulfilled his role as the oldest of the house by providing for his whole family, his mother would come to love and respect him. That's the reason why the children of neglectful and even abusive parents cannot let go of these parents later in life: it's that very hope that if they work hard enough for it, such parents might learn to love them in the end.

It is difficult, as children, to understand that some people simply do not have the capacity to love, or that the so-called affection such parents may exhibit later on in life is not real love or genuine interest, but rather a twisted expression of their own codependency.

But the eldest son was no fool. In fact, he was quite clever, and it wasn't too long before he realized and reluctantly accepted the discriminatory way that his mother dealt with her children. When his mother told him she couldn't afford to send him to college, he gave up an offer from a top private university to go to a less prestigious one that offered a scholarship, and all throughout his college years he studied hard and worked desperately at several part-time jobs to keep himself afloat and also give money to his parents. After he graduated, he gave his first paycheck and bonus incentive to his mother, who then used it to buy his younger brother a car and a suit, which is what she also did with the pay his sisters, who were not sent to college and got jobs right out of high school, brought home as well.

What finally made him angry beyond repair was when he began to discuss wedding preparations with his parents, in the midst of which his mother suggested they use some of his wedding fund that he'd saved up to buy his younger brother an expensive watch. He didn't talk to his parents for fifty years after that.

The departed mother loved her second son until she reached her deathbed. To her three daughters, she bequeathed the small apartment she had spent her final years in. It was in an old building, and the ceiling leaked; it was far from downtown, had no subway line nearby, and was in a neighborhood with no profitable gentrification potential. Everything in the apartment was breaking down; it would be better to sell the land share attached to it instead of taking on its maintenance. The cash deposits, stocks, dowry jewelry, and any asset that wasn't the house—everything useful, in other words—were left to the second son. There was no mention of the eldest son. He had been forgotten or was deliberately left out. Until the day she died, the departed only asked after her younger son and did not even mention her eldest.

The three daughters had lived their whole lives in neglect, and so they were equally uninterested in their parents or brothers, and thought that the way the will had been divided up was typical of how their mother had treated them their whole lives. If anything, they were a touch astonished at the fact that they had been remembered at all in the will.

None of them wanted to be the one to contact the eldest son. It was obvious to the three sisters how their oldest brother would react if, after all these years of silence, he were asked to head the funeral rites. It would be better if he refused to come at all, for there was no way of knowing how their two brothers would behave if they ever met again.

In the end, the departed's youngest granddaughter, who was the only one on speaking terms with the eldest son, called him and got him to come to the funeral. The three daughters had expected that there might be a fight. But in the end, the fight happened for unexpected reasons.

The departed's second daughter, when she got married, lived the closest to their mother, and therefore had taken care of the mother the longest.

This second daughter came to the funeral and laid down a handkerchief in front of her siblings. She informed them that her their mother had asked her to have this handkerchief cremated with her remains after her death. None of the departed's children had seen this handkerchief before, but because the second daughter had been the one to take care of their mother the longest, the eldest son and other daughters agreed to carry out her wishes without much thought.

The one who adamantly opposed this was the younger son, who happened to have arrived late to the funeral to boot. He insisted the handkerchief was his. Wasn't he the one who had talked to their mother the most, the one to whom she had given every object of value that ever passed through her hands?

And yet he had never seen this handkerchief before either, so therefore it could not have truly belonged to their mother, and it could not be cremated with her. Aside from the forced logic of this argument, the younger son in truth liked the handkerchief and the other siblings knew that he was vying to take all of her assets, right down to the smallest handkerchief, upon her death.

The handkerchief was indeed a pretty thing, a clean white square with a flowering bough and a little sitting bird embroidered on it. The fabric was thick and had a subtle sheen, and even those who knew nothing of thread counts and such could see it was some pricey material like silk or satin. The embroidery was in bright colors, which normally would look very old-fashioned, but here the colors served to make the flowers and bird vividly lifelike, made as they were with great skill and from thread as subtly lustrous as the fabric. The quality of the embroidery was truly like nothing that could be seen today on mass-produced articles and was clearly the work of a master of the craft.

As beautiful as it was, however, the other siblings wondered why a grown man would want a colorful woman's handkerchief embroidered with flowers and a bird.

Before they could ask this out loud, the eldest son

attacked the younger son, and the two men, one in his seventies and the other in his sixties, had a proper fistfight over a handkerchief that their mother in her nineties had left behind.

The real reason for the fight, however, was of course how their deceased mother had discriminated between her children, which resulted in a resentment that no amount of aging could erase. If anything, such resentment had accumulated with age, to the point where there was no way to resolve it.

The daughters tried to calm their brothers, but they were divided as well. The second daughter insisted they needed to follow their mother's wishes. The youngest daughter was more concerned with getting through the funeral rites without further disruptions and said they should just give the stupid handkerchief to the younger son and forget about it. The eldest daughter had seen so many variations of the scene before her play out, time and again, that she felt sick and tired and wished her horrible younger brother would just drop dead, but she kept silent out of respect for her mother. As the two sons fought for the title of Most Beloved Son one last time, the daughters had their own disagreement, without coming to a conclusion, and in the chaos, one of the grandchildren, the son of the eldest son, slipped the handkerchief into his backpack, then tore his father away from his uncle and took him home in the middle of the funeral rites.

In most ghost stories, this is the point where the handkerchief would start all sorts of mayhem. For example, the eldest son could be driving his father home when the sun suddenly drops over the horizon and they are stopped on the road by a woman dressed in a white sobok dress, her straight black hair flowing over her face down to her waist, her voice creepily demanding her handkerchief be returned, whereupon the son would stop and get out of the car to talk to her, and her neck would suddenly snap to the side or he would realize she had no legs under her skirt.

But no such thing happened. Instead, the eldest son ranted and raged at his son, presenting a litany of all the injustices his younger brother had brought upon him. His own son listened and drove in stony silence. The rage turned to lamenting, and when he arrived home, the eldest son took the handkerchief from his son's bag and threw it into a dumpster in the parking lot of his apartment building. That was his final blow to his mother and his younger brother. Neither he nor his son gave another thought that night to that handkerchief.

After his older brother had been dragged away from the funeral, the departed's younger son put on the black armband with the two stripes that the head of the household wore for funeral rites and felt good about having risen to this position in the family, but once he'd been harangued by the funeral center employees and his sisters about managing the remains and the funeral portrait and the address book to make the announcements, he shoved all the head of household duties off to his sisters and their husbands and went to an empty room in the center to lie down.

Even the irresponsible have their worries.

He was pushing seventy and everything he had wanted had been given to him by his mother, but now that she was dead, who would be there to make his every expressed desire magically materialize before him? He couldn't exactly get a job at that age, and if he were to work, he wanted to own a business, and he had such a plethora of surefire ideas as well, but he would need capital for that.

But his one credit line had just died, and he had run so many get-rich-quick schemes into the ground that his aging sisters were highly unlikely to scrape together money for him like his mother had. No one in the family would care for him now, as everyone hated him, and all he had left was to die alone.

He pitied himself to tears.

After a bit of sobbing and sniveling, he remembered the handkerchief his mother had left behind.

Women's objects had never interested him, but

that item was truly pretty, made by clever hands and surely worth some money.

Why had his mother asked his sister to burn it along with her body instead of leaving it to him?

He coveted it because it was a pretty object, and even more so as it was her last remaining possession. But most of all because for the first time, here was an object his mother had specifically wished not to fall into his possession. The colorful embroidery hovered like a ghost before his eyes.

He got to his feet and went around the funeral center, grabbing his sisters and asking them where had the handkerchief gone.

His sisters ignored him. As much as they and their husbands had expected another fight to break out because of him and his losing interest in the responsibilities as head of household for this funeral, it irritated them no end. Why hadn't he stayed in that spare room where he would at least not bother anyone? The sisters were so tired of having dealt with him for over six decades that they had no patience or energy left for him.

He ended up back in the empty room, where he sulked about and called his own eldest son. His son did not answer. After about five attempts, he gave up. He wondered if his nephew, his brother's son, would answer, but he'd never had his nephew's number in the first place.

The departed's eldest son had fallen out of contact with the younger son a long time ago. The younger son had known the eldest son had married and had children, but knowing it would then be expected of him to remember the children's birthdays and to give them New Year's money, he never made an effort to approach his brother's family.

But as he lounged about the unused room of the funeral center, he couldn't stop thinking about the satin-like fabric and the beautiful embroidery of the handkerchief.

He called his brother, and someone picked up.

"Hello, older brother. Are you never going to talk to me again?"

"Hello, Uncle." It was his nephew. Well, surely it would be easier to reason with his nephew than his brother.

"Ah," said the departed's younger son, secretly relieved, "I was about to call you . . ." His voice trailed off as he realized he did not remember his nephew's name. To cover up this lapse, he took on a scolding tone. "How could you have left without properly taking leave? Who raised you?"

"What do you want?" The tone of his voice suggested

that his nephew was sick and tired of him and very keen on hanging up the phone and never speaking to him again.

The departed's younger son hastily asked, "What did you do with the handkerchief?"

"What?"

"The thing your grandmother left," the younger son explained. "You know, the thing, the white satin handkerchief with the bird and the flowers embroidered on it. I looked everywhere for it, did you take it?"

"I threw it away," the nephew said curtly.

"You did what?"

The sound of the child's father's voice came over the phone from behind him. "Your mother died, and all you can think about is some handkerchief?"

His nephew hung up.

"You bastard! You thief! It doesn't even belong to you, why would you throw it away? Bring it back to me!" the younger son shouted into the phone, but again, his nephew had hung up. He called again, but neither his nephew nor his brother picked up.

The younger son got to his feet and paced the room, cursing, but it was no use. They continued to refuse to pick up, and eventually, his calls went directly to voicemail.

The younger son decided he would drive to his

brother's house himself and demand to be told where the handkerchief had gone, but then he realized he didn't know where his brother lived. Immediately in his mind, he blamed his brother for isolating himself from the family in anticipation of his mother's eventual death, just so he could attempt an inheritance grab without having taken care of her in the end—not that the younger son himself had done anything for her in her final years.

He vowed he would get that handkerchief by any means necessary.

The younger son ended up being kicked out of the funeral center by his sisters and their husbands. He kept asking the mourners where his brother was living, and then at the coffining ceremony had rifled through his mother's shroud in search of the handkerchief, this on top of his sisters already worrying that he was going to try to steal the funeral money, a very real possibility they'd kept in the back of their minds. The sight of him desecrating his mother's body drove them over the edge, and they came together as one to drive him out of the funeral center and their lives. Only when the funeral center security guards came running at the sound of his screaming about the handkerchief was he finally expelled from the premises.

No one had realized he'd been haunted by the

handkerchief yet. The second daughter forced the younger son into a taxi, threw in some taxi money, promised several times she would call him when the handkerchief turned up, and soon the taxi was on its way, the sister hissing to herself, "Has that bastard lost his mind? Why is he so obsessed over that handkerchief?"

This was an important question—more important than she realized—but the family was too busy with the funeral rites to care about anything else, and the departed entered the cremation chamber in the presence of her children and grandchildren but without the handkerchief.

No one wanted to think any more about the younger son, and no one even thought about the handkerchief. They needed to pay the funeral center, thank the mourners for their condolences and funeral money, and get a certificate of death so they could get the departed's final affairs in order at the district office, such as paying off her utility bills.

In short, there were many errands to run after a funeral, and none of them had the wherewithal to even think about handkerchiefs.

The younger son, throughout his life, had married three times, and only in the first instance did he hold a wedding. With the other two, they only did the paperwork.

This first wife was introduced to him through

his parents' friends, as it so often happens, and they dated for a bit before entering a marriage that lasted not three months before this wife came running back to her mother's house. The reason was that not only did her mother-in-law visit the newlyweds' house every day and dig through her fridge and laundry and inspect her son's clothes and sheets, she also refused to go home at night and instead insisted on sleeping in the master bedroom with her son while his wife was expected to sleep in the spare room.

As this was in the days when divorce often irrevocably ruined women in terms of reputation and finances, the practice at the time was for couples to hold a wedding and live together for a while before deciding to legally register the marriage at the district office. As evidenced by the fact that she had spent two years at a famous women's college, at a time when so few women went to university at all, the young woman had grown up in a progressive household where she was respected and educated to a degree that was rare for someone of her time, and she also happened to have a sharp mind and a clear-eyed view of the world.

Still, her mother was shocked that her daughter would try to give up her marriage. She tried to convince her daughter to try again, as divorce would mean living like a ghost in her childhood home, but she became even more shocked when she heard that the mother-in-law had insisted on sleeping with her own son every night, while her daughter was banished from the marital bed. The young woman's older brother went to her husband's apartment to get her things, and thus this first marriage of the departed's younger son was erased from his memory.

The younger son was now free. His mother was his private fountain of money, and there were women everywhere. That's how he met his second wife, and by the time he brought her home, they had already registered their marriage at the district office and a baby was growing inside of her.

The second wife was, compared to the first one, quite savvy, and offloaded most of the household chores on the mother-in-law, who insisted on visiting every day, under complaint of a difficult pregnancy. Her main occupation was figuring out how to use her husband to milk as much money out of her mother-in-law as possible. One couldn't call her the most ideal wife and mother, but she did have a certain way of handling people and could watch out for herself, which meant she deftly managed the bizarre love triangle between herself, her husband, and her mother-in-law, even as she weathered the storms of pregnancy, childbirth, and caring for a newborn.

This triangle fell apart when she learned that in the course of his going around doing "business" with his mother's money, her husband had also been going out with a variety of women, also with his mother's support—and this while she had been pregnant, as well.

Unlike many women in a similar situation in her era, the second wife of the departed's younger son did not turn a blind eye and endure it. She declared that, if anything, she needed to set an example for her child. She retained a lawyer, got her divorce and alimony, and made a clean break. Her mother-in-law did not try to stop her, as the child her second son's second wife happened to give birth to was a girl. The younger son never reached out to his daughter, and his ex-wife never reached out to him, and no one knew what became of this mother and child. The younger son occasionally, very occasionally, wondered if the child had been a boy, would his mother have made an effort to keep him? Would *he* have made an effort to keep the boy? He couldn't be sure. That was thirty years ago now.

Many women passed through the younger son's life after that, and this third wife he was with now was not with him for love or desire or even to display his virility or economic means, but because the match happened to be convenient for the both of them. The younger son, after his mother had become too old to be active anymore, needed someone to do the household chores, and his current wife had needed someone to provide her with housing and an allowance.

This third wife was also twenty years younger than him, but he himself was pushing seventy, which meant she wasn't exactly flush with youth herself. When they first met, she had claimed she was a childless widow, but after they began living together, it turned out she had a child whom she would sneak some of her allowance to, which her husband overlooked. They had never married, which meant no divorce proceedings would ever be necessary, but it also seemed like a huge annoyance to have reached their age and to quibble about who should get what in a split and—more important—if she left, he would have to find someone new to take care of him. Now that his mother was gone, they needed to live out their twilight years with what he'd inherited, and he no longer had the generosity to ignore her squirreling away his money for someone else's child.

Was it time to let her go as well? The prospect made him glum.

But then there was that handkerchief. The third wife was a woman, and as a woman, she might know where one needed to go to find such a thing, or at least something similar. He decided to task his third wife to look for such a handkerchief.

Less than a month later, he woke up to find that

his third wife had left the house, taking his bankbook, signature seal, ID, and all of his late mother's jewelry with her.

But this all happened later. First, the younger son came home the evening of his mother's funeral to find his third wife sipping tea and watching television with a young man. She called him her nephew, but judging by the tense look in their faces, he determined this was the son his third wife had kept hidden from him all this time.

"Come on, say hello," his third wife awkwardly urged the boy. "He's the man in charge around here. He went to his mother's funereal rites, so I assumed he'd be late . . . Look, I was frightened of being alone, so I called my nephew. You know how it is these days, it's such a violent world . . ."

His wife kept making the situation more awkward by offering up increasingly mendacious excuses for why the young man was in his apartment. The young man stood up and bowed. He hastily put on his coat.

"Why go now, stay a bit longer," said the departed's younger son, out of courtesy.

"Oh no," said the young man, "you have a guest and everything. . . . I'm sorry for putting you out . . ." His voice trailed off.

"Guest?" said the departed's younger son. "What guest? This is *my* house."

His third wife said, "Guest? Is someone else here?"

"There, the person you came in with . . ." The young man craned his neck toward the door. The third wife looked too.

There was no one there.

"Huh? Just a moment ago . . ." He was clearly agitated and his eyes darted about the room. Then, he quickly zipped up his coat and rushed to put his shoes on by the door.

"Thank you for having me!" He bowed, and before the departed's younger son could say anything, he was gone.

That was a prelude for what was to come.

The next day, the younger son's third wife happened to wake up early, at dawn.

She lay there in the dark, somewhere between dreaming and wakefulness. In her dream, she had been walking up a mountain path in search of something, an object she could not remember when she woke up, but in any case, a very important object in the dream. But no matter how much she searched that mountain it remained elusive, and the path became steeper without ever showing signs of going down.

The third wife called out to her husband, the departed's younger son, who was following her. In reality, they were in what the courts would call a common-law marriage, but in her dream, he was her own son. She needed this son's help to find that lost object, which was why, in her dream, she called out to him, and there he was, walking toward her in the dark, his vague form getting clearer, until she could see that he was carrying someone on her back. A woman, in a long, white dress, the folds of the skirt whipping and wrapping around her husband-son's legs, hindering his progress up the already difficult mountainside.

The third wife went up to him and tried to unwind the skirt from his legs, but then the woman on his back raised her head at her.

"Get it out," she said. Then, she screamed, "GET IT OUT!"

The blue face and the flashing green teeth in her mouth scared the third wife awake.

She stared at the ceiling as she caught her breath, then turned to her side to check if her husband was still asleep.

A woman in white lay between her and her husband. Her hair, as well as her skirt, was long enough to wind around her legs.

Just as the third wife slowly looked up from these legs, unsure if she was awake or still dreaming, the woman in white turned around to face her.

A blue face, a mouth full of green teeth.

The third wife screamed as she jumped out of bed. She slammed her hand against the light switch.

"What . . . what's going on?" said the departed's younger son groggily.

The third wife's eyes darted around the room. She threw aside the duvet. There was nothing under it except her husband. Her very annoyed husband.

"What's the matter with you? I was asleep."

The third wife managed to calm her breathing a little and said, "N-nothing. . . . It was just a dream."

"Turn the light off," said the younger son, irritated, as he lay down again and closed his eyes. Shaking, the third wife turned the light off in the room. It went dark. The white form she had seen was not there anymore.

She sighed. There was no way she was getting back in that bed.

Without making a sound, she left the room, carefully closing the door behind her. She came out to the kitchen. She turned on all the lights and sat down for a moment. Then, she got up and began to wash the rice.

A week after that, the third wife went to see a shaman. Her husband kept nagging her about finding some handkerchief. At first, she didn't understand what he was saying, so she bought a few at a department store. Her husband had flown into a rage and said these were not it. Apparently, he wanted a specific handkerchief—but how was she to find such a thing? She tried searching the Internet and asking around in stores and markets, but there was no handkerchief like the one her husband described. He nagged her day and night about it, and she became more and more exhausted.

Plus, her dreams were getting worse. There she was, climbing the mountain or up a tree or the stairs of some crumbling building, climbing and climbing with no destination in sight. And if she ever looked back, that woman in white with the blue face and green teeth, her skirts wrapped around her husband's legs, was coming up from behind. Her husband kept scolding her about finding something that was on the top of the mountain or tree or building, and the clothes or black hair of the woman on his back kept winding around his legs more, preventing him from moving, taking him downward. If she ever approached to try to extricate or help him, the woman on his back would scream *"GET IT OUT!"*

And the third wife would be jolted awake, panting.

And as soon as she opened her eyes, she would lock eyes with the woman in white.

The woman lay between her and her husband, staring at her. The white clothes that had once wound around her husband in the dream were now wound around her own body, along with the woman's black hair. She wanted to scream, but she could not open her mouth or move her body. The woman with the blue face slowly crawled over the third wife's body. There was nothing the third wife could do about it. She could not even close her eyes. The blue-faced woman whispered something in her ear. The voice was horrifying and those green teeth grazing her earlobe were even more so, whispering more and more rapidly but without raising her voice—the third wife could not understand a word this woman was saying. She wanted to cry for help to her husband, but he was fast asleep with his back to her.

"Wife."

Someone shook her. Her eyelids flew open.

"Wife."

She screamed.

"What is wrong with you? You kept mumbling and I couldn't sleep . . ." Her husband shot her a dirty look.

"Wh-what did I say?" She was still panting.

"I don't know. You were dreaming something." He lay back down and immediately began snoring again.

The shaman the third wife went to wasn't famous nor had she been introduced to her by someone, it was just some storefront that happened to catch her eye. This shaman was also not a real shaman but a con artist. It's important to point out that distinction here. The shaman had put up a sign with all the right religious imagery and whatnot, but she herself had never received the gods, was uninterested in matters of spirituality, and had never had a premonition in her life. She made her living by pretending to listen to the laments of the people who visited her and ripping off their money. Business was good, as she knew exactly what to say, such as what she said as soon as the third wife walked in the door.

"Your husband is seeing some woman!"

It was a truth well-known to her, thanks to her long experience, that any woman of a certain age with such a glum face was bound to be suffering from this same issue. There were, of course, still the occasional sufferers who had money troubles or issues with their children, but the married women of this generation tended to be savvy and knew how to get the information they needed, which meant solvable problems normally were directed to actual professionals. But there were still, even in these enlightened times, philanderers' wives who would visit a shaman before a divorce lawyer, that old cliché of "keeping the family together" continuing to hold some sway. Maybe, in the moment you've just realized your husband is a philanderer, it's extra difficult to admit that the family had already been broken apart.

The third wife did not confirm nor deny it—she was simply flummoxed. Strictly speaking, her husband wasn't having an affair. She just couldn't understand who this blue-faced woman was and why she saw her in her dreams every night, stuck to the back of her husband.

The con-artist shaman quickly gauged her reaction and shouted, "But the other woman is so young!" For that was statistically the case.

It struck the third wife that she wasn't wrong. It was impossible to tell the age of a woman who has a blue face, but that long black hair did make her seem very young.

"Is there no way to get her off his back?" she asked. This was the question the con artist had been waiting for.

She wrote her a talisman slip. It must be reiterated that this shaman was a con artist and there was no effectiveness to this piece of paper, other than some psychological reassurance for the one watching her write it. If it works, the con artist can say it was thanks to the talisman, and if it doesn't, she can claim that "This demon must truly be a wicked one" and offer the upgrade option of a goot ceremony. If she could get several expensive goot performances out of this one client and really milk her dry, that would be most ideal.

Surprisingly, the talisman worked. The third wife slipped the talisman into her husband's pillow when he was not looking, and she wasn't haunted by nightmares again—she could sleep deeply.

But there was a side-effect to this talisman. It brought about the opposite of what the third wife wanted.

Her husband would now wake in the middle of the night and wander outside.

At first, the third wife didn't realize what her husband was doing, she was too busy catching up on sleep that wasn't tinged with nightmares. But then one morning, after a good night's sleep, and having sent off her husband with a good breakfast, she was making the bed when she noticed the sheets were smeared. There was trash all over her husband's sleep clothes and stains that smelled like sewage.

Alarmed, the third wife immediately threw everything into the wash, not giving herself a chance to determine where the dirt had come from. She thought of asking her husband that evening about it but didn't. All her husband wanted to talk about whenever he opened his mouth was the handkerchief—the reason he went out at all that day was to go looking for it—and she did not want to set him off. And any talk of trash or sewage was unpleasant by default. Her husband was in a bad mood anyway, having suffered another failed day of searching, so she managed to persuade him, through his ramblings, to have his dinner and go to bed.

The next morning, she woke to find her husband out of bed, and out of the whole apartment. This time, there was trash and sewage everywhere, in the bed, in the wardrobe, trailing all around the threshold of the bedroom. The third wife cleaned once more, and as she did the laundry, she decided to stay up to find out what was going on with her husband at night.

He came home late that evening.

His clothes were sweaty and there was a sour, unpleasant smell about him, and he looked exhausted. Refusing dinner, he collapsed into bed, not even going on his usual rant about the handkerchief. His clothes were so messy and smelly that she was about to say something to him, but thinking something was going to happen that night, she kept her mouth shut.

She decided to wait.

She placed a chair next to the bed to watch over him and eventually dozed off. When she awoke with a start at the sound of rustling, her husband was getting the covers off of himself and leaving. The third wife waited a little so he would not see her, then followed him out the half-open bedroom door. Her husband did not put on his shoes at the foyer and simply pushed open the front door and walked out in his socks that he'd worn all day and hadn't taken off when he collapsed into bed.

The third wife quickly put on her shoes and followed. He did not take the elevator down but walked, a little unsteadily, down the stairs. After briefly questioning herself, the wife took the elevator down and hid in the shadows near the building entrance, still wondering why she was even doing all this. Before she could talk herself out of whatever "this" was, her husband appeared coming out of the stairwell and walked out of the building, still a bit unsteady on his feet. He went straight for the recycling corner of the parking lot, opened the dumpster, and began digging through it.

"Not here . . . not here . . ." he mumbled as he dug. "*Get it out . . . get it out . . .*" mumbled another voice at the same time.

It was this second voice that made the third wife freeze, and kept her from trying to stop him. Her husband continued to dig through the trash, and the strange voice continued to mumble.

He then suddenly straightened up and began staggering off in another direction.

The third wife agonized over whether she should follow. It was the middle of the night and peaceful, as this neighborhood usually was at this hour, but tonight it was especially quiet, not a single car passing by. The most sensible thing would be to try to wake him and take him back inside, but the thought of the strange voice held her back.

Some other choices occurred to her: she could also go home and pretend nothing happened and wait for her husband to return, maybe trying to get him to see a doctor in the morning, or . . . she could grab everything she could manage and leave him for good before he returned.

This was the first time it had occurred to her with such clarity that she could be on her own.

She'd resigned herself to taking care of him in his old age, but she hadn't bargained for said old age to look like this. This went beyond the scope of normal care.

Still, she took a deep breath, wrapped her arms tighter around herself, crossed the parking lot, and followed where her husband had gone.

The third wife found him only after walking for an age around the neighborhood. He had ended up in an alley outside their own apartment complex. He was crouched there, rifling through a filled regulation trash bag that someone had left out for the sanitation workers under a telegraph pole.

She called out his name. He did not look back at her. She called out again.

He half-turned his head. His eyes were unfocused and shone yellow. He drooled from his mouth as he mumbled, "It's not there . . . it's not there . . ."

Blue faces appeared in the air around him and chorused with her husband, *"Get it out . . . get it out . . ."*

The third wife took in a sharp breath. Her husband

turned to face her directly, and the blue faces, behind him, also stared her in the eye.

They said, "*Get it out . . . get it out . . .*"

The blue faces bared their green teeth.

The third wife turned and ran. She crossed the entire width of the apartment complex in a flash and was so out of breath, she made mistakes twice trying to input the lobby key code. As the doors slid open and she ran inside, she slammed her palm against the elevator button, but when it took more than a moment, she bounded up the stairs to their apartment instead. As soon as she was inside and had the manual lock fastened on their digital door lock, she collapsed in the foyer and caught her breath before calling her son.

As he groggily picked up, she screamed that she would explain everything afterward but right now, he needed to come pick her up *immediately*. The third wife was normally a sweet and demure woman, and the son had hardly ever heard her scream or seen her so terrified. He got up and was soon on his way.

Until her son arrived, she kept her grip on the door handle as a myriad of thoughts went through her head. The biggest and most overwhelming thought was the fear that her yellow-eyed husband would bring the floating blue faces inside her house. Why did she have to call her son—he might run into them and be harmed! The image fed her panic. She needed to let go and start packing, but she couldn't help thinking that the second she let go of the door handle, those yellow eyes and blue faces would push into the apartment.

The thought sapped the strength from her knees and she couldn't get up.

Her son arrived, and her yellow-eyed husband had still not returned. Only when she could hear her son's healthy, normal voice calling her outside the door could she breathe properly and open the front door. He came in and asked her what was wrong, but she only gripped his hand and trembled.

As they gathered her things, the third wife returned very quickly to reality. She knew very well where her husband stored his bankbook and signature seal. He distrusted mobile banking apps and was too lazy to learn computers, but more than anything else, his only source of income—his late mother—had also never used a cell phone or the Internet. This meant all of her husband's financial affairs were conducted manually. Her husband would go to the bank with the bankbook and ATM card and seal, or she herself would go in his stead. It had taken a long time for him to trust his third wife with it, but once he did, as the third wife was an honest person and always very precise with money, he eventually left all the bank chores to her. Consequently, the third wife knew exactly how much money he had left. As she opened the safe and took out the bankbook and seal and the jewelry his mother had left him, she took a moment to look at the ugly, if valuable, gold chains and rings and thought about how she had never owned such things in her life.

The third wife had been born to a poor family and married, at a young age, to a poor man who died in a workplace accident. To survive and raise their young son with the measly compensation she received from her husband's workplace, she became a street vendor. She was often extorted by two-bit street gangs, harassed by district office workers, and whenever her business started to pick up, they would smash up her cart and she would have to start again, or the district office would try to shut her down and she'd end up physically fighting them off. Eventually she had to quit. She worked in factories and did cleaning work in restaurants and motels and managed to raise her son and send him to college. He got a job, and she finally had some space to breathe, which she used to get a caretaker license. She took care of various senior patients for a while until she met her husband, while taking care of his mother. At the mother's recommendation, she became a kind of live-in housemaid to them both. Even after she was dubiously promoted from housemaid to common-law wife, nothing really changed aside from the fact that she slept in the master bedroom now. That, and the fact that she could handle the banking affairs.

The key difference between being a housemaid and a wife was the amount of severance payment either job would entitle her to. The unspoken agreement was that she would take care of him in his old age and provide hospice care in exchange for inheriting some of his money. There had been no discussion about when she would get his money nor how much, at that, nor did the third wife ask. She knew her position was at least that precarious. Several years had passed under a haze of vague promises and hopes, but the husband never gave his third wife any money or presents beyond what she needed to survive and take care of him. To him, she was just a housemaid he slept with.

But it is important to point out that she took care of him for a long time, and that the third wife knew she had more than enough grounds to claim a common-law marriage. There was talk back then that the inheritance laws would change to exclude siblings from automatic entitlements, which meant everything her husband had could end up belonging to her. Then she could give her son the expensive foreign car her husband drove, buy him a house when he got married . . . She had allowed herself to dream about this for at least a little bit, to have that sliver of hope on the otherwise dark horizon of what lay ahead for her—everyone has the right to dream, to hope for a better future.

This future did not include a husband who herded a bunch of horrific blue faces around as he rummaged through dumpsters at night.

The third wife grabbed everything of value in the house and a few changes of clothing and toiletries and left the house. Remembering at the last minute, she grabbed the car keys he always tossed onto the shoe cabinet when he got home.

And so, the third wife left, forever, with her son.

My sunbae stopped the story there. I waited. She didn't speak for a while.

"That's it?" I asked, impatient. "What happened after?"

"What do you mean?" she answered, smiling.

"The younger son, what happened? And what's with the handkerchief? Is the blue-faced woman a ghost? How did she become a ghost? And get *what* out?"

My sunbae laughed. "Please! One thing at a time."

The first person who was contacted by the authorities to come collect the departed's younger son was the daughter he had thrown away three decades ago.

This daughter stonily listened for a few minutes

before realizing that they were asking her to be responsible for the man who had more or less tossed her in the trash on the day she was born. She snapped back that she didn't know anyone by that name and hung up on them.

More people were called. The person who eventually came to pick up the departed's younger son was his youngest sister.

He had become almost unrecognizable in the short time since she'd last seen him. His face was gaunt, his eyes unfocused, his hair turned completely white, and even half of that had fallen out, revealing a bald crown. He was barefoot and smelled rotten and wore a ripped suit.

The neighborhood people had caught him digging through their trash and he'd been taken to a facility. He held a piece of cloth to himself and kept mumbling strange words.

"What's that? And what is he saying?" his sister asked a worker at the facility after the initial shock had died down a bit.

The worker shook her head. "It's a handkerchief or something. He refuses to let go of it, so we just let him keep it. He gets really violent if you try to. . . . Anyway, he keeps saying something about getting something out, but we don't know what."

The youngest sister stared at the object her brother

was holding onto once more. It must've been white at one point, but it was so dirty that it was now a dark gray.

When he noticed her staring at it, the brother screamed, "GET IT OUT! GET IT OUT! OUT!"

She couldn't take him in like this. The youngest sister looked up care homes she could put him into and called up her siblings, but they were all sick and tired of their brother and said there must be some money left over from their mother, which the youngest sister, upon going to his house, found out to be untrue.

And that's where a completely different and a much more ordinary type of family story began, one that is not a ghost story, but perhaps the scariest story of all.

"What happened to the handkerchief?" I asked my sunbae.

"It's in Room 302," she said without batting an eyelid.

"Room 302?" I was puzzled. "What's Room 302?"

"Room 302 of this institute. We literally just walked past it."

As I began to turn around, my sunbae added, as if she weren't blind and could see, "Don't turn around. If you look at her in the eye, she'll follow you."

I froze mid-turn.

"She'll follow you even more if you covet it," continued my sunbae. "It's better to have not seen the handkerchief at all."

My sunbae began to walk again, slowly and leisurely.

Hastily, I followed her. I wanted to look back, but I was too afraid. I relied on the beam of light from the torch to keep me facing forward, trying not to give in to the desire to look back and also to run, as I slowly followed my sunbae down the hall.

Cursed Sheep

DSP—let's call him by his initials—ran a streaming channel that specialized in ghostly spectra and other paranormal phenomena. He applied for a job at the Institute because of this, actually, as he hungered for content more than he had ever hungered for ghosts or monsters and the like. He kept his reasons for applying a secret, of course.

On the first day of work, my sunbae, as she did for everyone, passed on some guidelines: that he did not need to go into every single lab room, that he only needed to check if the door was locked; that if he heard footsteps in the hall, he should ignore it; and that he should never look back or talk to anyone he sees.

DSP only regarded her cautions as more fascinating content fodder to add to his video streaming. Once he took over the shift from my sunbae and she went back to her room, DSP took out the phone he had hidden in his pocket and briefly considered live streaming before deciding instead to film where he was with the help of his flashlight. He stopped himself from launching into a narration about where he was as my sunbae could've still been in earshot.

He decided to go up a floor. As he climbed, he whispered into the phone about where he was, why he was there, and what kind of video he hoped to film.

He opened the stairwell door and entered the floor. As he turned his camera down toward the corridor, he almost dropped his phone.

Someone had appeared in the middle of the hall.

"You can't come in here."

DSP tilted his flashlight on the face of the man who now blocked his path.

"You can't come in here," the man repeated. "Who are you?"

"I work here. The question is, who are *you*?" DSP tilted his phone and checked in the corner of his eye that the camera was capturing this. "Aren't *you* the person who can't come in here?"

The man in the corridor did not answer.

DSP continued to record with one hand and swept the flashlight up and down over the man who blocked him with the other. The man wore a very ordinary suit. The name tag on his chest flashed in the light of the flashlight, so he couldn't read the name. Not that DSP had intended to read it with any care.

"I said, who are you?"

The man didn't answer. He turned and began to walk away.

"Hey!" shouted DSP.

The man didn't answer or slow down. DSP held out his phone with one hand and his flashlight with the other as he ran down the corridor after him. "Stop right there!"

The man vanished just as abruptly as he had appeared.

"I am currently running down a corridor of the Institute as I follow a suspicious man!" shouted DSP into his phone. He came to a stop in front of the door the man had disappeared in front of. He put his flashlight in his mouth and tried the doorknob. It was locked.

The doorknob was the round, old-fashioned kind, the same as all the others on the doors of the floor, of the whole building, for all he knew.

DSP sat down in front of the door. It would be impossible to pick the lock while filming with one hand and shining the flashlight with the other. He put the flashlight down on the floor and switched on the flashlight on his phone. He held his phone with his mouth by the phone grip as he tried various ways of opening the doors that he'd seen in Hollywood movies or TV dramas.

The old-fashioned doorknob opened easily with the edge of a credit card.

DSP put his flashlight in his pocket and continued to record video with his phone as he entered the lab room.

The lab was very ordinary. He found the light switch next to the door and the room lit up in fluorescent light.

There was a steel desk right next to the door with a shelf that had two or three books on it. On the opposite wall from the door was a window that had its blinds drawn. Under the window was another desk and chair.

On that desk was a reading lamp, an alarm clock, and a single white tennis shoe. And nothing else.

DSP whispered narration into his phone as he approached the desk under the window.

"I am picking up the tennis shoe. It has a cartoon drawing of a sheep on the vamp—that's what they call this part, the top part under the shoelaces—but the size seems to be for an adult. A rather mischievous grin on the cartoon sheep. The material isn't rubber, it's some kind of fabric, something that feels like wool. Maybe it's one of those sheep wool sneakers that used to be popular. Something about them being good for the environment? They're expensive. I only see one of them here."

He put the shoe down on the desk. There was nothing else, really, to film in that room.

DSP opened the window blind, which rolled up with an ordinary *rrr-rrr* sound. Disappointingly, no ghost appeared in the window, nor was there anything extraordinary outside. The window was protected with security railings. There was only darkness beyond.

DSP lowered the blinds and was about to leave the lab when he then paused.

He picked up the shoe.

It had been fun when the man appeared out of nowhere and vanished like smoke, but this experience had been a letdown after that.

DSP decided to make a video around living a day with the shoe inside his house to see what happened.

Nothing happened.

Not while he drove home with the shoe in the passenger seat. Not after he got back and slept during the day. Not while he ate his dinner-breakfast.

How many more days did he need to have it with him? The lab might find out and make things difficult for him.

DSP searched for *burglary* on the Internet. The information on what such a charge would entail made him uneasy. Well, he would go to work with the shoe. If they seemed like they were looking for it at the Institute, he would quickly put it back where it was.

If they hadn't seemed to have caught on, he would bring it back home and keep it for a few days more.

Nothing happened, once again, at work.

My sunbae did not ask DSP about the shoe. All the other workers had left work by the time he came in. He did not run into the suited man again on his rounds. The Institute was just dark and silent and boring.

DSP wondered if he should try going into the other labs. He had asked my sunbae on his first day whether they had security cameras.

"We have a few on the first floor and in the parking lot. Nowhere else."

"Really?" This surprised him. "Not even on the floors with the labs?"

"Especially not on those floors. We did for a time, but they kept breaking down."

DSP liked this explanation very much. Which was why he was disappointed that nothing had happened to him when he had stolen what he'd assumed was a haunted object.

Now he felt nervous. If nothing continued to happen, there would've been no point in his getting a job at the Institute. He could try breaking into another lab and stealing something else. But that would be pushing his luck—surely the Institute would begin to notice if things kept disappearing on his shift?

Which was why he decided to keep the tennis shoe for a few more days and put it back before finding a new object.

DSP never put the tennis shoe back where he'd found it. Because he couldn't find the place where he'd found it.

In his memory, the lab in question was above the employees' lounge, up the stairwell that was at the far end of the corridor. That floor above was where he had run into the suited man and had chased him down the corridor to a door on the righthand side. But he couldn't remember which door it was.

He took out his phone to check which door appeared in his recording.

The recording was not there.

Amateur mistake. DSP felt annoyed with himself. He had to press the record button one more time at the end to save the recording, but he must've forgotten to do that when he closed the camera app. He should've done a live stream instead. And he would've, if he hadn't been worried that my sunbae or the suited man would find out his intentions. But now that he thought about it, live streaming himself being dragged out of the Institute by the suited man would've garnered some views for his channel if anything, even better if the police had come running.

Such regrets. Live stream only from now on, then. And he must mention to his audience how the video "mysteriously" disappeared from his phone.

DSP took the tennis shoe back upstairs. This time, there was no suited man. He went down the corridor trying each righthand doorknob.

They were locked. That's right—he'd forgotten about that.

He tried opening one using the credit card method with which he had easily unlocked the round doorknob the last time. That didn't work either.

As he kept trying with the other doorknobs, the alarm he had set on his phone sounded. He had to go back to his watch duties.

DSP went downstairs.

As he made the rounds on the other floors, he wondered what he should do now. Maybe something strange would happen if he took the shoe on his rounds?

After he did the rounds down to the first floor, he went back up to the floor where the employees' lounge was.

There was no longer another stairway at the other end of the corridor.

DSP took out his phone and the shoe and began to live stream.

Urgently, he whispered the whole story of the mysterious suited man, his stealing of the shoe, and the entire floor that suddenly seemed to have disappeared.

His audience response was lukewarm. Only a very few viewers seemed enthused.

DSP asked them what he should do with the shoe.

Most of the people who answered said he should keep it. And that's how the shoe ended up in the passenger seat of his car again as he drove home.

When he opened his door, all of the small objects of his home pointed to one place.

He didn't notice, at first, because the larger furniture like the bed or the desk hadn't moved. But the shoes in the foyer were all pointed toward the door. The utensils were out on the counter, and the heads of the spoons and the wider end of the chopsticks all pointed toward the front door. Cups on the table had fallen on their sides and were also pointing to the door. The bathmat in front of the bathroom was turned to face the front door. Every pen and pencil and his computer mouse on his desk were turned toward the door as if waiting for him to come home.

DSP was not the observant type, so it took him a while to notice these changes. Only when he saw the pillow was laid vertically on his bed did he begin to feel something was off. He couldn't recall what position his pillow had been in when he left, but surely it wasn't like this, perfectly vertical and pointing straight at the door.

He called his mother, who lived two hours away from him by bus. As soon as she picked up, he shouted at her about coming into his apartment without permission. His mother shouted back saying she hadn't.

Only when DSP hung up did he think this may be the work of a burglar. He was torn between checking to see if anything was stolen and live streaming what was happening.

In the end, he decided to do both. He put his phone on a selfie stick and began to stream and check for anything that was missing.

That day's understated paranormal phenomena live stream reached record numbers of views. The more he showed how everything was pointing toward the door by opening drawers and cabinets and so on, the more his eyeball count grew. Most of the viewers accused him of doing it all himself just to get more views on his channel, but they still watched him go through the things in his room. There were people gleefully commenting about how messy his apartment was, as well as the people who kept spamming the word "FAKE" in the comments.

These viewers numbered more than the sincerely

curious ones, but it didn't matter. DSP only cared that he had a high view count. And there were a few who were genuinely fascinated.

As he found nothing was missing, DSP concluded the live stream saying this proved that it wasn't a burglar but poltergeist activity and ended his broadcast with a satisfied feeling before collapsing into bed.

He woke up at the sound of his phone ringing.

His eyes not quite open yet, he prodded the side of the bed for his phone and picked it up. "Hello."

"*Where would you like for us to send the funeral wreath?*"

The voice was a normal office voice, brisk and formal. DSP was confused.

"Hello. What?"

"*Should we write the standard 'Our thoughts are with you' on the ribbon?*"

"What ribbon? What wreath?" DSP was beginning to wake up. It occurred to him that it could've been a burglar after all and what was stolen was in fact not an object but his private information, and now they were buying things using his credit card.

Only about a quarter awake, his brain struggled with this new and unwelcome thought. "Wait. Who—who are you? Someone ordered a funeral wreath?"

The voice on the phone ignored his question. "*What time will you board the hearse?*"

"Hearse?" DSP sat up. He couldn't remain lying down any longer.

In the same even tone, the voice said, "*You must arrive half an hour before your scheduled cremation.*"

"What? Who are you!" DSP's voice grew louder. "What is this, a prank? I'm going to find you and kill you!"

"*If you would like to proceed with the burial, we can send you the shroud with the coffin in the same delivery.*"

"Who are you! Who told you that you can call this number!"

"*Would you like a funeral portrait and incense with that delivery?*"

"Die, you fucker!" DSP shouted with all his might.

He hung up, and seething with rage, he threw his phone on his pillow. This did nothing for his rage, so he got to his feet and was about to throw his phone on the floor when he stopped.

He thought of his highest view numbers ever from the night before. He thought of all the videos and photos that were stored in the phone. With great difficulty, he managed to calm himself down and lower his arm that held up the phone.

He looked in his call history. The number was there. DSP called it.

"*The number you have dialed is not in service. Please hang up and try again.*"

DSP hung up and this time, dialed the number on his call history himself, extra careful that he got every digit correct.

"*The number you have dialed is not in service. Please—*"

He hung up.

That's when he remembered, with a glad rush, that his phone was set to record all phone calls. He quickly swiped through his screens for the app, and with fingers trembling, tapped it open.

There was indeed a file for his last phone call.

He pressed play.

"*Hello.*"

That was him. He couldn't hear the other voice at all. DSP raised the volume on his phone.

"*Hello. What?*"

He still couldn't hear any other voice than his own. DSP raised the volume to maximum.

"*Wait. Who—who are you? Someone ordered a funeral wreath?*"

Instead of a voice answering, he heard a thud. Then, another thud. Like something hitting a hard floor.

"*What? Who are you! What is this, a prank? I'm going to find you and kill you!*"

His recorded voice, violent and amplified, rang in the room.

A small voice whispered, "*Why don't you try?*"

DSP jumped. He paused the playback. He scrolled back a few seconds.

"I'm going to find you and kill you!"

"I said, why don't you try?"

The small voice was a little clearer then.

DSP tapped pause.

He scrolled back again and listened for the third time.

"Who are you! What is this, a prank? I'm going to find you and kill you!"

"You're the one who'll be killed."

Then, the small voice softly cackled.

DSP closed the app.

For the first time, he began to feel genuinely frightened.

Until he had to leave for work, DSP agonized over whether he should erase the recorded file.

Without a doubt, he would need it for his live streaming—if the recording changed every time he played it, that would make for some amazing content. But the very thought of that small voice, especially with that cackling at the end, made him want to erase it immediately.

All throughout the drive to the Institute, he kept glancing uncertainly at his phone and the white tennis shoe in the passenger seat.

It was more profitable not to erase the recorded file.

But it was probably best to return the tennis shoe to the Institute.

Yes—that was what he would do. If he could not take it back to the specific lab room he found it in, then he'd leave it in the employees' lounge or the bathroom or wherever someone else might pick it up and take care of it.

He arrived at the institute and parked the car in the underground parking lot. He got out of the driver's seat, went around the car, and opened the passenger seat door.

The tennis shoe was not there.

DSP couldn't believe it.

He felt under the passenger seat, then under the driver's seat. All that came up were old receipts, tissues, pebbles, dust, sand, even a dried leaf, empty cans and plastic cups, used straws, an empty bag of snacks—no tennis shoe.

He opened the back seat door. On the back seat were his selfie stick, tripod, ring light, microphone, equipment bag, cables, spare batteries, and various out-of-season articles of clothing.

DSP took out each item one by one. Still no tennis shoe.

He checked the trunk. Because he had taken out the equipment in the back seat to put in the trunk, there was nothing in there except an empty water bottle.

There was no tennis shoe.

DSP stared into the trunk.

It had to be at home. It simply had to. He must've taken it inside with him to use in a live stream and got sidetracked by all of his things pointing at the door and the phone call he received and forgot about it.

This self-explanation verged on desperation more than logic.

A burst of loud music startled him.

It was the ringtone on his phone. He opened the door of the passenger side.

My sunbae was calling him. Reassured at the prospect of hearing a living human's voice, and with some dread about what this call might be about, he answered his phone.

"I'm about to sign off for the night, where are you?" she said. *"Is something the matter?"*

"No, no," he said reflexively, "I'm in the parking lot. I'll be right up."

"All right." My sunbae hung up.

DSP stared at his phone. He called up the recording of the call just now and played it.

My sunbae's voice and his had been recorded normally. There was no strange voice or weird cackling. This was a relief.

He headed for the elevator.

The stairwell only lit up when there was movement detected. On this day, of all days, he did not want to face a dark stairway. Or the lights failing while he was still on the stairs, like in a horror film.

"You can't come in here."

DSP screamed.

The man had suddenly appeared before him, blocking access to the elevator.

He wore an ordinary suit, had an ordinary face, and spoke in an ordinary voice. There was a name tag on the breast pocket of his suit. DSP was not in a state where he could look too carefully at the name.

DSP took a step backward and shouted, "Who are you!"

"You can't come in here," the man in the suit said in his usual tone.

DSP turned and ran.

He came up to the stairwell door, flung it open, and ran inside. There was a small window in the stairwell that looked out into the parking lot, which was brightly lit.

He couldn't see any man in a suit there.

A loud racket pierced his ears. DSP winced and looked down at his phone.

It was my sunbae. He picked up the call.

"Hello? Where are you?"

"Sunbae . . . Sunbae, help me."

"What? Why? What's going on?"

"A strange man . . . keeps . . . I can't find the

shoe . . . the phone . . ." The words refused to cohere into sentences in his mouth.

"*A shoe?*"

"Tennis shoe . . . sheep drawing . . . the lab . . . not there . . . can't find it . . ."

"*Are you still in the parking lot?*"

"Yes." DSP began to sob.

"*Look,*" said my sunbae, "*just come up. I don't know what's going on but come up and we'll talk this through.*"

She hung up the phone.

DSP breathed deeply. He began to climb the steps.

The stairwell lights switched on when they were supposed to.

There was no sudden plunge into darkness, nor lights flickering on elsewhere in the empty stairwell. A bug crawled next to his right foot.

At first, he ignored the bug and kept climbing. Something, though, made him look down again and there was the bug once more.

It was larger than before.

DSP was about to step on it when it quickly moved away from him. He was about to chase it but gave up and continued to go up the stairs.

Just a few flights more, and his eye caught the movement of a small black thing by his foot. The bug was even larger than before.

At first it had been a speck, then it was the size of

a fingernail, and now it was about a third the size of a little finger. He really needed to step on it now.

DSP raised his right foot.

On his right foot was the white tennis shoe that had disappeared from the passenger seat. The line drawing of the sheep on the vamp grinned at him.

DSP screamed. His scream echoed.

He ripped the shoe off his foot and threw it down the stairwell. He began to run up the steps.

He was soon out of breath.

With an elevator shoe designed to boost his height on his left foot and just a sock on his right, he felt seriously unbalanced at the hips, and the concrete step was freezing and painful on his almost bare sole. He had to stop midway, doubled over and out of breath, and saw the bug was now two-thirds the size of his little finger.

He could make out a small head and little legs. It stood on its back legs and reared up.

DSP raised his right foot. It occurred to him that he was only wearing a sock on it, but that didn't matter. That bug had to die. The triumphant satisfaction of the bug getting crushed underfoot would be worth the mess.

His foot came down. The bug darted away. DSP stomped and stomped, all over the stairs, but the bug escaped every time.

It was infuriating. He bent down and observed

where the bug had pattered off. The bug also crouched and stopped moving. DSP kept his eyes on it, waiting for the perfect time to strike.

The stairway lights went out. He was shrouded in darkness.

DSP screamed. He flailed his arms about.

Then the lights came back on, much to his relief.

Now was not the time to waste his energy on bugs. DSP refocused his thoughts toward one objective: he had to get out of the stairs.

Loud music echoed in the stairway, and he almost dropped his phone down the stairwell. It was my sunbae.

"*Where on Earth are you? What's taking you so long?*"

"I'm going up the stairs right now," he said, half-sobbing. "I don't know where I am . . . I'm on the stairs—"

"*Shall I call the deputy director for you? Shall I tell her to come to the stairwell?*"

DSP was stuck.

If the deputy director got involved, he would have to confess to stealing the tennis shoe, to live streaming from the Institute, and even to getting a job there under false pretenses. He could get sued. And he wouldn't be able to live stream from the Institute anymore. Just when he was getting some hits, when the viewers seemed to respond to this sheep tennis shoe business, when he was about to stream the voice recording and this endless stairway . . .

His thoughts got this far when he suddenly felt he was being watched. He turned his head to the left.

On the landing of the stairway above sat a sheep.

DSP stared.

The sheep stared back.

Its wool was messy. It was far from white, more of a dirty gray-brown. There were patches that had been shorn off here and there, with large, exposed wounds on the places where the wool had been shorn to the skin, glowing red under the stairwell lights.

DSP held up his phone. He turned on his camera app and began to record.

Slowly, he began to walk up the stairs.

The sheep sat on the landing and continued to watch DSP and the camera lens that was trained at it.

There was another sheep on the next landing.

Its wool was also gray and dirty, with patches shorn off in spots. Different spots than the previous sheep's, with different wounds.

There was another sheep on the landing after that. The sheep were large, and the stairways narrow. The sheep, however, did not seem uncomfortable.

They sat and blankly observed DSP.

When DSP saw there was yet another sheep on that next landing, he looked up the stairwell and saw, as far as he could see, there was one on every landing.

And there was that bug again, next to his right foot. It was definitely larger than it had been.

DSP raised his right foot. It darted away just in time.

He exhausted himself trying to stomp it out. He stared at the bug instead.

It stood on its hind legs and waved its front legs in the air.

Or were they arms? It seemed like such a human gesture. He looked closer at it.

It was not a bug.

It was a human the size of a finger.

DSP jumped back.

The stairs were narrow, and he instinctively looked behind him. A sheep sat on the landing below, looking up at him with its black eyes.

DSP looked down again. The bug-human was waving their arms at him.

"What are you?" DPS whispered. "Why do you keep following me?"

Instead of answering, the bug-human moved their arms about in an incomprehensible gesture. Tired, DSP raised his right foot again, and the bug-human ran away.

DSP saw he was now wearing the white tennis shoe on his right foot again.

He took it off. He threw it at the bug-human. The bug-human avoided it. The tennis shoe tumbled down into the dark below.

"Damn," DSP mumbled as he watched.

Thud.

The sound came from below like an answer to his curse.

Thud.

It sounded like something falling on a hard floor.

Thud.

DSP realized something was walking up from below.

When he turned and began to run up the stairs, he heard a soft cackle in his ear.

DSP was completely out of breath as he ran up the stairs.

There was another landing. He expected a sheep to be sitting there. But instead of sheep, there were two doors, side by side.

The one on the right was closed and had a lit EXIT sign glowing green above it. The left had no door at all, just the white doorframe. There was a corridor beyond under white fluorescent light that weakly spread out into the landing.

Without hesitation, DSP ran through the left doorframe.

A shadow passed over him and he looked up. The heel of a large, white shoe threatened to stomp down on him.

DSP managed to avoid it just in time.

The white heel came down toward him again. DSP desperately did everything he could to avoid it. He tried to go back the way he came, but there was only a white, hard wall behind him.

The doorway he had come through was gone.

His back against a tall white wall, the white heel rising again, DSP looked around for a place to escape. And that's when he realized it.

He was on a large, white stair. If he wanted to get up to the other stair, he'd have to scale a wall that was as tall as he was.

His hands gripped the slippery white edge of the stairs as he heaved himself up with all his might.

The giant heel was about to come down on him again.

"Stop!" he shouted at the huge white tennis shoe. "Stop it! I'm a person!" He waved his arms. "I'm not a bug! I'm *you!*"

But the heel had no mercy.

He leaped to the wall again, and just as he was about to climb, he realized he should be going the other way—that foot in the air had no interest in listening to him, so why was he chasing it? No matter how many desperate steps he climbed to plead with the giant foot—for what, to be picked up? To be saved?—all that foot seemed interested in was to stomp on him once to kill him.

It was easier to go down than up. And below, in the parking lot, he had his car.

Carefully, he began to climb down the wall-like stair. And he slipped.

He fell into a deep darkness.

My sunbae ended up calling the deputy director, who discovered DSP sitting in the stairwell by the parking lot. He held his cell phone in one hand and a tennis shoe in the other, shouting about sheep and bugs. The deputy director tried to approach him and talk to him, but DSP swung his arms and screamed at her not to step on him. The deputy director called DSP's family.

His mother and older sister came and took him away.

"So what happened after that?" I asked my sunbae.

"He discontinued that paranormal live streaming channel," she replied simply.

This gave me pause. I then asked, "But how do you know this?"

"Know what?"

"With Sook and Chan, I can understand that they

told you their stories. But this live streaming guy, he couldn't have told you all those details?"

"When he called me about being in the stairwell, I heard a bleating behind him," she answered.

She did not explain further.

And I did not ask anything else.

Silence of the Sheep

The deputy director has a pleasantly relaxed demeanor, and a right hand with only a thumb and no other fingers. When my sunbae went on vacation, the deputy director subbed in for her shift. As we sat in the employees' lounge, she told me the story of her life, back when she used to live behind the veterinary school of a big public university. That's where, she told me, she had become haunted by a sheep.

The deputy director had lost all the fingers on her right hand while working a machine in a factory. They had become so mangled in the machine that the doctors had to amputate them. After her recovery, she became too afraid of machines to go back to factory jobs.

Nightmares had plagued her the whole time she

was getting treatment. The deputy director was also right-handed, which meant it was very difficult for her to find a job she was suited for. Her meager compensation and severance pay dwindled as her medical and living expenses accrued.

To make matters worse, her husband had fallen into an online gambling addiction after her daughter had left for college. There seemed to be some connection between these two events—her daughter getting into college and her husband developing a gambling addiction—that she couldn't quite understand to this day, something to do with his resentment over the success of his own child.

Her husband, like many a gambling addict depicted in movies and dramas, threatened her and beat her as he demanded money from her. Their daughter, who was home for the holidays at the time, happened to witness this. She tried to stop him, and the husband hit her as well. That's when the deputy director finally called the police. As he was dragged away, he screamed at the deputy director that her remaining fingers were just as useless as her missing ones and that she was better off selling them and her other body parts for money.

Her daughter begged her to divorce him. The deputy director had to agree. She initiated divorce proceedings and fled the marriage.

Her daughter returned to her university in the city. The divorce case would drag on until her graduation. This suited the deputy director, if anything. It gave time for her daughter to finish her studies and find a job, and she herself could start her new life as a divorced woman.

She just had to survive until the divorce came through. There was still some money left over from her worker's compensation, but she wanted to pass that on to her daughter. Divorcing her husband meant she would have no more legal obligation to him, but dissolving the legal relationship between her husband and their daughter was a different proposition altogether. The deputy director was most fearful that her former husband would bully and harass their daughter, and then he would pass on his gambling debt to her. There was also the not-insignificant danger of him selling their daughter to human traffickers.

She didn't want to think such a thing was possible, but then again, until he became addicted to online gambling, the man had never been violent toward his family. One just never knew.

But on the list of things the deputy director *did* know was that any debt her ex-husband went into would have to be shouldered by her daughter. She already had some experience in this regard; she had taken on her older brother's "business debt" when their mother had come to her in tears, asking her to do so. Though once the deputy director got married and was considered part of someone else's family, her brother had to find someone else to shoulder his debt.

There was also that older cousin who spent her entire life paying off her father's debt. As soon as this cousin got her associate's degree, she was thrown into the workforce meat grinder as her father went from failing at one "business" and then the next "business," until his daughter's credit was ruined beyond repair. He was now in his seventies and still begging his daughter to bail him out.

The deputy director also had an aunt whose life's work was paying off her husband's debt—the reason she got saddled with that was because the older brother of her husband had stolen all the money of the household and disappeared. Her aunt's mother-in-law knew where this thief-son was and what he was up to, but she refused to tell anyone. Thus, debt flowed downward like sewage to the weakest members of the family, and those thrust into the role of cleaning up this sewage were more often than not women—daughters, daughters-in-law, mothers, and granddaughters.

Sayings like "an eldest daughter is an asset to the household" or "mothers with sons die on the road while pulling a cart" basically mean the same thing.

Only by sucking the marrow dry of those most vulnerable in a family can that family be maintained. Which is why, no offense to Leo Tolstoy, most unhappy families tend to be unhappy in similar ways in the end.

The deputy director did not want that kind of life for her daughter and became determined to find a way to separate her husband and her daughter as much as possible, which was why, even after their divorce, she remained in the city she had lived in with her husband. It was so she could keep an eye on him and stop him from looking for her daughter.

And she had to find a way to make a living in this town.

There wasn't much she could do with so many of her right-hand fingers missing. She had lots of experience and wasn't that old, but everyone took one look at her right hand and shook their heads.

After many failures, someone suggested she become a fortune teller, which she laughed off at first. But the person recommending this said this didn't mean she should receive the gods in a shaman ritual or whatever—she could learn about tarot and Saju and other fortune-telling skills and set up a little vendor tent on some busy street, which was all the rage at the time. The recommender added that she knew of someone who had saved up enough that way to buy a small condo. All the necessary skills could be learned at the local learning annex for free, and she wouldn't need both hands to do it. She could dramatically fan out tarot cards with her left hand with some practice.

And that's what she did. It was a little annoying doing the Saju calculations with her left hand, but the deputy director practiced diligently, and she became adept enough.

What was even harder than learning how to use her left hand was dealing with people. She wasn't very extroverted and did not exactly have the gift of gab. She had worked long enough at a factory that made packing material to know just about everything on how such things were made. This was her first time in a customer-facing job, and she was selling something that had nothing to do with packaging, to boot. She was supposed to provide some mixture of therapy and a vague sense of hope by garnering quick trust from her clients, which felt like she was conning them. This was difficult for her.

She lived at a goshiwon hostel behind a university's veterinary school at the time, as she'd heard from many that she needed to be near young folk to make a success of this venture. She had no money to set up a proper tent, which is how she came to take her tarot cards and Saju books and a portable chair and table to set up wherever there were many pedestrians until some store owner or passing cop chased her away. Then, she would find another place to set up.

She made very little money, and it took a long time for her to set up her things with her injured hand. On some days, she spent more time roaming around with her table and chair than she did actually doing readings.

She went into the university a few times. Oddly enough, no one stopped her. Apparently it was a public university, and as such they were legally obligated to keep the campus open to the people of the city. If she set up her table and her cards, campus security came running, but as long as she didn't unfold her table or show her cards, they left her alone.

The deputy director would sit in her portable chair on a quad and watch the students go by. She thought of her daughter. At the very least, she had managed to send her daughter to a good school like this one. She had visited it many times, and whenever she thought about her daughter, pride swelled in her heart.

If only she could see her more often. But at least the distance between them meant her ex-husband would have trouble bothering her as well.

There were always sheep grazing in the bushes around the veterinary school. It was a surreal sight. The green quads, the modern university buildings, the large signs with the important-sounding names of labs and other facilities—between them all were the mazelike roads and shrubbery where the sheep nibbled or sat on the grass.

The sheep were covered in wounds. Their wool was shorn bald in different places, and there were surgical-looking wounds in those spots. Some of the sheep had one or both eyes that were bloodshot, and others that had some kind of painful-looking object heavily weighing one of their ears down.

Fascinated at first, the deputy director was soon horrified to learn that not one of those sheep were unscathed. Some of them even trailed long catheters behind them.

The sheep never moved away from her when she approached, either because they were very tame or had simply gone through too much to care about any random human. They sometimes made sounds like gnashing teeth. Perhaps they were angry at the humans who had wounded them so.

The thought frightened the deputy director, and she did not approach the sheep after that.

Then one day, the sheep came to her at her goshiwon. And that's how the sheep began to follow the deputy director.

The goshiwon was rumored to have been built over a pit where the veterinary school had buried the animals they had experimented on. At least, according to the students who came to get their fortunes told. Maybe because of the association of tarot with the occult, the students liked telling her ghost stories like that. A student added that of course they followed all the proper legal procedures in burying the animals. No one wanted the school to appear on the news for a bunch of dead animals being dug up from some nearby construction site. The school would be shut down, the students all said, and people would go to prison. At the same time, they seemed gleeful enough to tell her about the ghosts of the many animals that had been sacrificed on the altar of science and learning.

The deputy director found this glee adorable. They made her miss her daughter very much.

The veterinary school students seemed to get attached to the animals they took care of. These animals had never harmed anyone, a student said to her, which was why he felt terrible for putting them through so much suffering. But it was necessary for their training, for them to go out into the world later on and treat countless other animals. Their bodies were very different from humans', of course, and they were unable to explain whether their symptoms improved or worsened after some treatments. It was a constant dilemma that in order to find a cure for animals at large, they had to harm these specific animals—a dilemma no tarot card, Saju interpretation, or her half-therapy could resolve for them. The only thing the deputy director could do was listen to them.

Perhaps it was because of these students' stories that she opened the door of her goshiwon room to the sheep that had come to see her.

The sheep had been standing there outside her door, red surgery wounds all over it.

Without a shred of suspicion, hesitation, or fear, the deputy director had stepped aside to let the sheep come inside. It didn't make a sound as it did so.

The deputy director went back to her narrow bed, which filled up almost the entire room. The sheep lay down on the sliver of floor space she had between the bed and study desk and quietly went to sleep.

When the deputy director woke the next morning, the sheep was gone. She thought nothing of it. Just as the sheep had come to her because it needed her, it had now gone to where it needed to be next. That was all there was to it.

But the sheep was not really gone.

Like always, the deputy director left the goshiwon that morning with her folding table and portable chair. She set them up across the street from the university gates where there was a row of stores.

One of the store owners came out and complained

that her table blocked the store entrance. As always, the deputy director apologized and began to collapse her table and chair, and for some reason, she suddenly said to the store owner, "Don't lend her that money."

"What?" said the store owner in surprise.

"I said, don't lend her that money." The deputy director stared at the sheep sitting next to the store owner.

"What money?" The store owner narrowed her eyes. The sheep next to her slowly shook its head.

"The store owner across the street," said the deputy director, "she asked you to loan her some money, didn't she? Her youngest son is going to lose it."

"And how would you know all this?" But the store owner's voice trembled a little.

The deputy director didn't notice. She was still staring down at the sheep by her feet. The sheep's eyes were swollen red, and there was a large surgical scar under its chin. The sight of this wound pained her.

"That youngest son, he's involved in some multi-level marketing scam. Don't lend him that money. It's not an investment. It's a con."

As if agreeing, the sheep sitting next to the store owner gave a nod. Then, it got up and walked away.

Leaving behind the aghast store owner, the deputy director picked up her chair and table and other things and followed the sheep.

For a short time, the deputy director became famous for her fortune-telling in that neighborhood by the gate of that public university.

The sheep might answer very frivolous questions but ignore very important ones. It seemed to treat the question of whether one would be late to a date at a bar or whether one's father would need heart surgery with equal importance and with the same calm equanimity.

What was unfailing about its answers was that it was never wrong.

The sheep didn't always come to help her. On the days it didn't show up, the deputy director had to make up whatever answer she could. The sheep appeared when it wanted to.

When the deputy director looked down at it in search for an answer, she would sense what it wanted her to say, and she would say it. Sometimes it was what her customer wanted to hear, and sometimes it wasn't. The sheep didn't trouble itself either way. Therefore, the deputy director didn't trouble herself either. She made money on some days and didn't on others. The sheep didn't care too much about it, so neither did the deputy director. When a customer occasionally got angry and cried or even threw things or shouted at her, the deputy director and the sheep would only gaze impassively at them. The customer would eventually realize she was not looking at them in any interested way. The deputy director and the sheep would continue to gaze as these embarrassed customers hastened away.

The deputy director learned many things through the sheep. The sheep were deliberately wounded by the veterinarians in many different spots and experimentally infected with different kinds of germs. Or the sheep would be fed with toxins. Once these deliberately-made wounds healed over, they were rewounded and reinfected. The life of an experimental animal was one of constant, unending suffering.

Still, the sheep did not wish for revenge, nor were they cursed. They only wished to be free from pain, to have a life free from suffering where they could graze in some meadow. It struck the deputy director that this was more or less the life that most humans wanted as well, and that filled her with pity.

One day, the deputy director woke up in an alley in the neighborhood across the university gate.

She smelled, and there were dirty brown clumps in her hair. She tried to get up. The entire left side of her body felt like she had been beaten there. She had been sleeping on the folding table and chair, using her tarot cards and other fortune-telling equipment as a pillow. Her wallet and phone were on the ground under the folded table, dirty with mud.

She turned on her phone. Four days had passed

since her last conscious memory. She could not remember at all what had happened in those four days.

The deputy director returned to the goshiwon. The manager was about to complain to her about her late rent when she took one look at the state of the deputy director and said nothing. Once she got her things back in her room, she showered and changed and opened her banking app on her phone to pay her rent.

At that exact moment, her daughter called.

"Hell—" The deputy director could not even get to the end of the word before her daughter began shouting at the other end.

"Mom, what happened to you? Why didn't you answer your phone? And what's with all this money?" She was practically sobbing.

The deputy director felt a wave of terror and dread as she tried to sound as normal as possible.

"I'm, I'm sorry, there were just so many customers recently—"

"And the money? Where did you get all that? You send me a huge amount of money and won't answer your phone, like some suicidal person! Do you have any idea how worried I was?"

"Sorry, I'm sorry, it just happened that way."

Her daughter kept interrogating her on what,

exactly, had "just happened." The deputy director could hardly answer that question.

She calmed her daughter down and managed to get her to hang up.

Then, she opened her bank app and looked at the most recent transactions. Two days ago, someone had sent her a sum of money that had a number and many zeros after it, in two installments. It was about three times her old annual factory salary. A big sum.

She had never possessed so much money at one time in her life.

The sender was not someone she knew. And the deputy director had transferred that money last night to her daughter.

There were seven missed calls from her daughter after that. It was better this was so, as she'd probably been in no state to receive that call. Who knew what she would've said to her daughter while haunted by the sheep.

The deputy director checked for other clues of her whereabouts from the last four days. There was no one else who had called her aside from her daughter. The money sender's name was not in her contacts or call history.

She wondered if she should rest for a few days, seeing as she was not in a healthy state of mind, or she could go back to where she had been fortune-telling to see if she could find the person who gave her that money.

All right then—she would go out.

If only to make sure this was not some trick of her ex-husband's to get to her daughter.

Like she normally did, the deputy director set up her table and chair in the neighborhood across from the university gates. She knew now to set herself up at the very edge of the sidewalk so as to not bother the store owners. It was very peaceful, and there were hardly any pedestrians about, much less customers.

The door of the store closest to her table opened a crack. The store owner poked out her head.

The deputy director felt nervous. In her experience so far, nothing good ever came from any of the store owners poking their heads out of their doors.

"Hey, I, uh . . ." The store owner did not finish her sentence.

The deputy director got up and began to put away her things. The store owner quickly stepped out and came up to her, which prompted the deputy director to hurry up.

"No, I meant to say, that thing with the lottery, can you do that for me too?"

"What?"

The store owner grinned awkwardly. "You know, you did it for that customer, the scratch-off lottery. She went and bought it where you told her to buy it and came running back to you all trembling and said she'd transfer you some of it as a good-luck payment, she took your bank details."

There was a place that sold lottery tickets down the street. The deputy director had never stepped foot in there. She thought of the large sum that had entered her bank account.

"Can't you, well, tell me where to look as well?" The store owner sidled right up to her. "Maybe the big lotto or the pension lottery, while you're at it? I'll pay you good-luck money too, if I win."

"When . . . when was that?" The deputy director's voice shook. "Who, who was the person? The one I told where to—"

"Oh, that person? I have no idea. She said you were famous on the Internet or something, for how good you were at fortune-telling. That she'd come to see you because of it, to prove it to her by telling her what ticket to buy. You pointed in that direction and told her to buy just one ticket from there. . . . That was amazing! If I had known you were that good, I would've asked you to tell my fortune ages ago!" She crept even closer to the deputy director. "Can't you tell me something like that? I let you put up your stuff in front of my store and never said a word. Think of it as rent, hmm?"

The deputy director quickly folded her table and chair. Without the use of her right hand, this was slow going, but she managed to get everything together.

"Hey, don't just go like that!" The store owner grabbed her arm. "Not after you took up this space in front of my store for so long! Come on, you owe me that much!"

The deputy director looked down at the hand that grabbed her arm. The sheep was sitting on the ground next to the store owner.

The sheep shook its head. It spoke through the deputy director.

"The sheep has to want to do that."

The store owner stared at the deputy director. But the deputy director stared at the sheep.

"And the sheep will no longer come to you."

"Sheep?" The store owner was confused. "Look, remember that time you told me not to loan my money, I really should've listened to you then, because that woman's youngest son really was part of some multilevel marketing scam. He asked me for a hundred million and I loaned him just half of that, but it looks like I won't get even that back.... Come on, help me out!"

The sheep lifted its head and looked up at the store owner. Its eyes were as bloodshot as before, and there was a fresh surgical wound on its neck.

The deputy director had a feeling that the borrower not only wanted to keep the half of the hundred million but would also come for the other half as well.

"You better check your locks from now on," the deputy director said. "He'll bring a knife."

"What?"

"He. Will. Bring. A. Knife."

The store owner's eyes turned dark. She let go of the deputy director. The sheep sitting next to her stood up.

Swiftly, the deputy director left the scene. As she ran across a pedestrian crossing, the light turned green to red midway and an oncoming car screeched to a halt, followed by a volley of curses. The deputy director ignored it.

She managed to drag all of her things to her room at the goshiwon, tossing them inside.

And with her hands still shaking, she took out her tarot cards and Saju book.

It was unforgivable, she felt, that she had given someone a lottery number.

Her ex-husband's gambling addiction had begun

through the lottery, simple tickets one could easily buy online.

Then her husband started with sports gambling, and soon enough, he had fallen into a downward spiral where the deputy director had ended up losing her family. She hadn't had the best of marriages, even before the gambling, but the life they'd built together was still all that she had known, and at least her daughter had been safe from debt.

And her husband had thrown all of that away, all those years of contentment, for his gambling.

The deputy director had no interest in the distinctions between legal and illegal forms of gambling—she became terrified that she was following her husband's path.

The path of addiction.

She stuffed her tarot cards and book back into her bag.

She couldn't just burn them like in a television drama, it wasn't as if she could find another job so quickly. She needed to have a plan before giving this up, and also a plan for what to do to exorcise the sheep from her. If possible, she also needed to find the person who had given her the money and return it.

She didn't want to take that money from her daughter—but how else would she get such a sum?

She began to have a headache.

She lay down on her bed.

The sheep entered her room and lay down on the floor again. The sheep did not wish for the human's unhappiness. The sheep had merely wanted the deputy director to be happy, which was why it had done what she had most wished would be done.

And this realization terrified her.

When she woke up, she was in a strange city.

A month had passed.

No matter what, she must not contact her daughter.

That was the first thing she thought when she woke up in a strange city. There was no folding table or portable chair with her this time, or even her wallet or phone. Her pockets only yielded bits of tissue paper and other trash. She had no ID or cash, nothing.

Her thoughts kept desperately returning to her daughter. But she couldn't be a burden to her again—and what could she possibly tell her, that she was being haunted by an animal and wandering all over the country?

It was after midnight. The bus terminal was dim. The deputy director found her way to a hall where it was better lit, but all the stores were closed and shuttered. Only their security lights were on.

What was she going to do now? She looked around and headed for the ticket office. Maybe there was a night-shift worker there. If she could just get a free ticket, she might be able to find her way back home.

Under the sign that said NIGHT BUSES was a ticketing window with a small light lit above it. A white screen stood against the window, however, and she could not see the other side. The deputy director stared at the sign and the English words MIDNIGHT TIMETABLE stamped in blue under it. Someone had written under this that "Night buses will be unavailable for the time being."

She had never been as devastated as in that moment.

Not even when she lost her fingers had she experienced such a breakdown of her soul. She dropped into a crouch and started to sob. No one came for her, even after she had stopped crying from exhaustion. The deputy director lay down on the cold terminal floor and fell asleep.

When dawn came and the buses began to run, she grabbed the first employee she could see and begged him for help. He called the police. The police called her daughter, and the situation unfolded in precisely the way in which she had least wanted it to. In the afternoon, her daughter arrived.

The sight of her mother not having washed or eaten properly in a month made her burst into tears.

As they headed for the daughter's city, people shot them curious glances, but the mother slept through almost the entire ride, waking up with a start from time to time. Only when she was reassured her daughter was next to her did she fall asleep again.

Her daughter was with her now, and there was no sheep.

It was decided that the deputy director would stay with her daughter for a while.

She showered and borrowed her daughter's pajamas and ate something, which did much to restore her. Meanwhile, her daughter reported her mother's phone and credit cards missing.

"You know, there was a call that came from your number," the daughter carefully said.

The deputy director felt something hard and heavy in her chest.

"I thought it was you at first, so I picked up," her daughter went on, "but it was a man I didn't know."

"Who? What did he say?"

"What was your name, where were you, that he would take your phone to you, so he needed your address."

"Did you tell him?"

Her daughter vigorously shook her head. "I would never. But then he asked me for my name and address, that he was going to bring the phone to me.

I was scared, but I couldn't block the number because it was yours."

The deputy director's passcode was so simple that it would've been easy to break. Thank the heavens she had stored her daughter's number as "my little girl" and not her name. Moreover, she did not use any kind of text messaging, choosing instead to write down her daughter's address and other important information in a small notebook, which thankfully the man who had her phone did not seem to have.

The deputy director sighed and hugged her daughter tight.

"Mom, just stay with me here," her daughter said while still being hugged. "The money you sent me, I didn't spend any of it. It's all there."

The mention of money made the deputy director's heart sink.

Her daughter reached for her hand and grabbed it. "So Mom, just be here with me. You've gone through so much. I've paused your phone and cards so all you need to do now is to rest for a while."

The deputy director stroked her daughter's hair. "All right," she said. "Let's just stay together."

And rest she did.

For a while, she did not even leave that one-room apartment. When her daughter left to go to classes, she cleaned and did the dishes and the laundry. She ironed her daughter's clothes, wiped the refrigerator, and made banchan and stew. Her daughter came back in the evenings, and they'd have dinner together, watch television, and go to bed early.

Those days with her daughter were pleasant and peaceful. The deputy director was reminded of their lives when her daughter was little, when she still had a job and would go to work at dawn or take extra late shifts to make ends meet, much to the neglect of her daughter. At least now, she could do some of the things she couldn't do when her daughter was a child. These were her thoughts as she ironed her daughter's clothes.

Then one day, the daughter said, "Mom, let's go buy clothes."

"Clothes? What for?"

Her daughter teasingly replied, "Are you going to wear my clothes for the rest of your life, then?"

"What's wrong with a mother wearing her daughter's clothes?" She stood up and struck a pose. "I bet everyone thinks I'm your sister."

Her daughter laughed. Then she turned serious. "But still, Mom, you should at least have some clothing you can go outside in and some shoes."

"Go outside? Why would I do that? I love being home." She lay down on the floor as if to make a point. "So comfortable."

Her daughter came up to her and pulled her leg.

"Come on, Mom, let's go shopping. Has it ever occurred to you that I want to go shopping myself?"

And so, the deputy director went to go shopping with her daughter.

And that's where she met the sheep.

The deputy director hadn't wanted to go to crowded places. Who knew what would happen to her, and most of all, she did not want some monstrous thing happening in her daughter's presence.

Meanwhile, her daughter was touchingly excited about going on a rare outing with her mother. She took her to the most popular shopping mall in the city. Chatting endlessly, they ate snacks together and looked at all the clothes and appliances. Soon, the deputy director felt calmer and happier.

The underground of the shopping mall was like a maze of shops. By the time they had made it through to the department store on the other end, the two were exhausted. They stopped at the department store food court to eat something and have tea. Across from the food court was a pop-up sale.

"Mom, let's see what they have over there."

"I'm tired," the deputy director said. "Can't we just go home?"

"You're home all the time! We've got to take in everything we can on this very rare occasion."

She dragged her mother to the sale section.

As they looked through the racks of out-of-season clothes, the deputy director and her daughter moved farther in, where they were selling shoes.

A pair of white tennis shoes caught the deputy director's eye.

She drifted toward them, and the salesperson next to the shoes rack came in for the kill.

"Yes, these shoes you see here are made from wool felt, using sheep wool, they're light and breathable and repel water . . ."

The deputy director was not listening to her. She was staring at the white tennis shoes that had a line drawing of a sheep with a mischievous grin on what the salesperson called the vamps.

"You like those?" said her daughter as she came up to her.

Instead of replying, the deputy director reached out and picked up the shoes. She looked at them intently.

"We'll take them," said her daughter. There was no need to check the size. The deputy director held these shoes that would fit perfectly on her feet and stared at them without a word.

"Are you all right, Mom?"

In a daze, the deputy director turned her head toward her daughter, who was gently rubbing her mother's shoulders.

"What? Oh. Yes. Come on, let's go."
They returned home.

The next dawn, the deputy director put on the shoes with the sheep on them and set out from the apartment. Her daughter was still asleep. She said nothing to her daughter, as it wasn't the deputy director wearing the sheep, it was the sheep wearing the deputy director. And that was how she returned to the bus terminal of the strange city.

"I was wondering where you'd run off to. Got all cleaned up?"

The deputy director opened her eyes. The face of a man she didn't recognize loomed right in front of her. He was lying on top of her, crushing her underneath him.

"Had a nice time at your daughter's house, huh?" The man groped her. "How old is she? Twenty? Twenty-one? She seemed young. In college?"

The deputy director tried to move, but the man she didn't know was too heavy. The more she squirmed, the more he bore down on her. "Hey, cut that out. Tell me your daughter's name."

She screamed.

"Go ahead." The man she didn't know smiled. "See if anyone comes."

It was dark around them, and the pavement she was lying on stank of cigarette butts and other trash. The deputy director screamed again. She could feel the man she didn't know putting his hand on her trouser zipper. She thrashed with all her might.

"Someone's been feeding you, look at how strong you are!" the man mocked. He began to strangle her. "Where does your daughter live? How old is she? What is the name of 'my little girl'? Tell me and I'll let you go."

She felt suffocated. She opened her mouth to scream but no voice came out. He suddenly let one hand go and raised it in the air.

But then the man began to shrink.

The deputy director was so surprised that she didn't realize what was happening as the man shrank to the size of a child, then her forearm, and then a baby. The man became so tiny that he stood on her breast and began to buzz like a mosquito, shouting something.

She picked him up by the head. The tiny man struggled against her pincer grip.

The deputy director got up.

A sheep stood next to her. It nodded to her. The deputy director put the tiny man she didn't know next to it, and the sheep sat down on him.

The deputy director dusted herself off and hiked up and zipped her trousers.

The sheep sitting on the man she didn't know lowered its head, indicating the ground. She looked at where it pointed with its snout. There was cash scattered about. The man she didn't know must've dropped it in his struggles.

The deputy director was not interested in why the man's clothes and everything had shrunk along with the rest of his body, but his money hadn't. She gathered it up.

Goodbye, the sheep somehow said.

"Be well," replied the deputy director.

She left the alley, which was behind the bus terminal of the strange city. The sheep, still sitting on the attempted rapist, calmly watched her go.

The deputy director returned home with only one shoe on her feet. She never found the other one again.

"I donated that one shoe to the Institute," the deputy director said. "Because it'll be safe here."

I nodded. What she said made sense somehow.

"How is your daughter?"

She smiled. "She's doing well, she graduated and got a job. Horrified her to learn I worked here, but I kept getting promoted, and now that I'm deputy director, I think she's accepted it now. That this is the best possible place for me to work."

The deputy director looked the happiest when she talked about her daughter. This made me happy, too.

The story doesn't end there.

The deputy director later learned that her ex-husband had died. Her daughter had been contacted with the news first, and she had told her mother. This ex-husband was found dead in that strange city the deputy director had found herself in twice. He hadn't eaten for a long time and was bone-thin, and his hair and teeth had almost all fallen out. He was lying in a small rented room, gripping a phone. It was his only possession.

"What happened to the phone?" I asked. Since it was the last possession of someone who starved himself to death because of a gambling addiction, it must be haunted by his dissatisfied spirit, which made it a perfect object of study for the Institute.

"The police have it," the deputy director said.

"What?"

"It was a burner phone."

She did not explain any further. And I did not ask anything else.

The deputy director looked at the clock. I looked

at it, too. It was time for my rounds, and for the deputy director to go home.

"I'm off to work. Goodbye."

"I think I kept going to that city because I wanted my ex-husband to die," the deputy director said.

Instead of answering, I nodded. I didn't know what to say.

"It's a good thing my daughter made it within the window to decline inheritance. She didn't have to take on his debt." She looked at me. "All right, I'm going home. Do your rounds and let me know if there's trouble."

"I will!"

The deputy director smiled and waved. I left the employees' lounge.

Blue Bird

It was an especially soporific day.

That was the problem with working at night. I read somewhere that no matter how many hours one sleeps in a day, a normal person has to be asleep at some point between one and three a.m. They do say the time between one and three a.m. are when ghost sightings are the most common. Maybe a lack of sleep during those hours makes people see things.

But it was my job, and I had no choice. After my rounds, I would go back to the employees' lounge. I usually wanted to drink a cup of coffee before I left work.

There was no one in the lounge today. A book was lying open and face down on the table, like someone had left it there in the middle of reading it. The title said it was one of those old historic books we learn about in school but translated into modern Korean. Its wraparound paper band declared there was a new timeline and afterword in this "enhanced" edition. This piqued my curiosity, so I picked it up and began to read.

This is the story of a country that fell to invaders a long time ago. A woman of high birth escaped its impending ruin with her baby in her arms. Her husband had been beheaded in front of his family by the sword of their enemies and their house had been burned down. The woman risked her life to save her child and ran through the forest, only for her path to end at the edge of a cliff with a river that raged below. As the forest echoed behind her with the shouts of the enemy soldiers and the thunder of their horse hooves, as well as the clash of swords against armor and the whizzing of arrows in flight, she stared down at the white water below. Just as she had closed her eyes and was about to jump, her baby moved. She opened her eyes. Her baby looked up at her with an innocent smile. As their gazes met, the baby gurgled and reached up for a lock of the mother's hair.

The mother could not kill her baby.

The hooves and the shouts grew closer.

She hugged her baby tight one more time.

"My child," she whispered as she embraced the baby in her wrapping cloth. "You must live."

She gently laid the baby in some bushes between two rocks, covered her mouth, and leaped into the river.

When the enemy followed the forest path up to the cliff, they found no one there—almost. Just when they were about to turn their horses around, they heard a child cry. A soldier with good hearing followed the cries and found a baby, wrapped in cloth, lying in the bushes. The soldier brought the baby to his captain.

"Leave it," the captain said. "It'll perish on its own."

The soldier was about to do so when the captain noticed the handkerchief around the baby's neck. It was white satin and embroidered with a flowering bough, on which a bird was sitting. Intricate, astonishing handiwork. He tried to grab it from the baby's neck. It wasn't easy, as the baby squirmed and cried. As the captain moved his hand around the neck of the baby to undo the knot, the baby scratched his hand.

The captain untied the handkerchief and ordered his soldier to lay the baby on the ground. He then moved his horse toward the baby to trample it. The hoof stamped down on the baby's left arm.

The baby screamed as if she had been burned.

"Die soon," said the captain.

The enemy disappeared down the forest path.

The baby continued to cry long after they were gone. The sun rose above the forest and briefly sprinkled down some light, but it was soon behind the trees.

As the shadows began to lengthen and the baby sobbed on, a pauper couple walked up the forest path. They had been foraging the forest for mushrooms, herbs, acorns, fruit, or anything else they could eat.

The couple had been born into poor homes and spent their lives wandering and knew all about the many kinds of suffering in this world. Which was why they couldn't ignore the crying baby abandoned on the mountain path. They took the baby to their hovel. When they took off the wrap to wash the baby and dress her wound, they noticed the embroidery on the wrapping cloth and realized whose baby this was.

The poor couple looked at each other.

The wife took the wrap and carefully folded it, making sure the embroidery didn't show, and hid it among their other clothes. Her husband lit a fire and boiled water. The couple washed the baby and fed her. They did not have much, but they gave the baby a warm hearth to call home.

The years passed, and people stopped mentioning the fallen country or even trying to remember it. The baby had grown into a young woman. Her left arm was twisted and shriveled, but she was renowned for her skill with the needle, especially her embroidery. Despite needing both hands to do her work, she could still use her left arm to hold the embroidery frame or cloth and nimbly work the needle with her right hand. She could thread the needle by placing it between the fingers of her left and finding the eye with her right, and she seemed to have no trouble making knots and matching colors of threads. Her fame brought her household sacks of grain, baskets of fruit, expensive goods, and shining silver coins. The paupers were no longer paupers, and they did not have to forage on the hillsides anymore.

One day, the servant of an important house came to visit, saying she needed to commission a handkerchief as a gift for a bride-to-be.

"Make it exactly like this one."

The handkerchief she presented was of white satin, intricately embroidered with a flowering bough and a bird, a most unusual item. The servant also brought forth some white satin and spread it before the young seamstress.

"Use this cloth," the servant said. "It was brought here from afar, so be careful with it. If you do a good job, the captain will reward you handsomely."

After the servant left, the couple who had raised the seamstress stared at the white satin handkerchief without saying a word. Then, they gave each other a look. The husband rose and went to the attic where he took down a locked chest. Hidden in the bottom of it, never unfolded since the day she was found until now, was the cloth the baby had been wrapped in.

They carefully spread it before her. The bloodstains on it had hardened, but the embroidered red flowers on the bough and the bird with the blue body and green beak were as vibrant as ever. Now they realized these were the symbols used in the regalia of a highborn family. They slowly explained to her that she was really the last descendant of an extinct noble house.

The young woman wordlessly listened to this story. She gently touched her withered left arm and the dark bloodstains on the wrap. Her fingertips brushed the embroidered flowers and the blue-and-green bird.

The bird flapped its wings against the white satin sky.

My child, the bird whispered. *You must live.*

She took a step back in surprise.

"The bird recognizes you, My Lady," said the woman who had raised her.

The words "My Lady" surprised her a second time as she stared at the couple. For to the young woman, it was these two, who had loved her and protected her and taken care of her, who were her father and mother.

"It is not as if I can restore my house on my own now," she said after a long pause. "But more than that, I do not wish to bring harm to my mother and father who stand before me by making claims."

The couple wept at the mention of "mother and father." And the family agreed unanimously that the best thing to do was to continue in their modest and ordinary lives as they always had.

But fate led them down a different path.

The handkerchief was finished much earlier than the time the servant had ordered. When her father said he would deliver it to the captain's home, the young woman insisted she would go with him. She had never done this before, and she could not say why she asked to do it now. Perhaps she wanted to see with her own eyes the enemy that had killed her birth parents and brought her country to ruin.

The house of the captain, from courtyard to the spaces between the pillars, was filled with baskets and coin chests. Servants bustled around preparing food and wrapping wedding gifts in colorful cloths or paper, which they placed in the baskets and chests. The captain's son sat in his room with the door open as he watched the servants make these preparations.

When he heard the handkerchief was finished, he ordered the young woman and her father to step into the inner courtyard so he could inspect it himself. And the sight of the young woman filled him with greed.

It was not love, nor was it even lust. The captain's son, like his father, was a cruel man. He glimpsed the withered hand by her side, and he had wondered what it would be like to disgrace such a woman.

This only son who was about to get married commanded the young seamstress, "Your father may go. You shall stay."

The young woman's father turned pale. Just as he was about to fall to his knees and beg, the young woman spoke first.

"Our household is but a poor one, and without my needlework, no one can bring food to my father's table or put clothes on my mother's back. I beseech you to give me leave."

"Then you shall be my concubine," said the captain's son. "Live in this house and do your sewing for the children who shall be born in this house, then neither you nor your parents shall starve."

"But that is absurd," said the young woman, who had to stop herself for a moment to calm her tone. "You are about to be wed, it is impossible for a low-born such as I to enter this household before your wife."

"How dare you speak to me this way!" the captain's son shouted. The servants stopped what they were doing and turned to look at what was going on.

"The great lady who shall be mistress of this house and the family she comes from will not be happy at this news."

This infuriated the captain's son. "Lock up this insolent wench and punish her!"

None of the servants stepped forward. A wedding was an auspicious event, and the captain had a reputation to uphold. Who would want to offend the bride's family?

An old servant stepped forward. "It shall go against our mores to accept a concubine before a wife. You must marry first."

"Who dares to speak to me that way!" the captain's son shouted.

"What's all this noise?" His mother came out into the inner courtyard.

The captain's son looked down on the whole world except his mother and father. As he cowered, the young woman and her father quickly made their way out of the captain's home.

The captain's son did not give up easily. He had never been denied what he wanted. This rare humiliation he had suffered made him determined to make the young woman suffer. At the earliest opportunity, he gathered his most trusted and cruelest servants and went with them to find the young seamstress.

That day, her father had gone to the market for rice and stew ingredients, and her mother to the cloth seller for thread. The young woman was alone in the house with her work when the captain's son broke down the little door of their home and strode inside as if he owned it.

"What is that?" he asked, pointing to a corner of the room. On the table was the wrap that the young seamstress had been found in. The young woman and her mother had carefully removed the bloodstains from it, which made the red flowers on the bough and the blue-and-green bird look more vivid than ever. The young woman had used the wrap's bird and flowers as a model for her work, for they were more intricate than that of the handkerchief she'd been given. The captain's son walked up to it and grabbed it.

"You stole the satin we gave you to make money somewhere else?" A distasteful grin split his face. "Thieves must be punished."

The servants were ordered to drag the young woman to his home, where they threw her into a dark storehouse. The captain's son tore the wrap and threw it down in front of her.

"I shall rip you apart as well." He laughed as the servants shut the storeroom and lowered the bar.

In the dark, the young woman felt around the floor and picked up the ripped pieces of the wrap.

You must live, the torn bird whispered to her.

The wedding preparations of the captain's son continued. The handkerchief the young woman had embroidered was sent to the bride in the neighboring village in a large chest along with other baubles. On the morning of the wedding, the bride wore the ceremonial robes sent by the groom's house and took the embroidered handkerchief in hand before climbing on board her palanquin. The bride's party set off.

As they made their way through the forest to go over the mountain, the trees began to rustle. By the time they passed the path that led to the cliff that overlooked the river, a flock of birds covered the sky and then swooped down upon the bride's palanquin. The palanquin carriers and the people trailing it were terrorized. No one was killed, but by the time the birds had left, the palanquin was covered in bird droppings and pecked and scratched and broken to the point where it could not be ridden anymore. In tears, the bride had to be escorted back on foot to her old home.

The servants at the captain's house had finished laying the wedding banquet tables and were making final preparations for the food. The captain's family wore their best ceremonial robes, and they all awaited the arrival of the bride. The people of the village also waited, their mouths watering at the sight of all the food. They waited a long time, but the palanquin did not arrive. The whispers began.

Instead of a palanquin, a messenger came through their gate. He told them of the flock of birds that had attacked the bride's party, strange birds with blue bodies and green beaks that had destroyed the palanquin and pecked and scratched at its carriers and passenger.

The news enraged the captain's son. "That thieving bitch used some kind of trickery," he shouted. "Bring her and her conniving mother and father to me, now!"

The servants rushed to the storehouse and dragged forth the young woman. The captain's son drew his sword and swung it around as he showed it off to all that gathered in the courtyard. The captain and the captain's wife looked at each other and at the spectacle before them, bewildered and confused.

"Thieving bitch!" the captain's son screeched. "You stole my satin and now you curse my wedding with your demons! Confess to your trickery!"

"I have done nothing," the young woman proclaimed. "It is your father who stole my country and my mother, and you who tried to disgrace me, which is how your house has earned the ire of the heavens."

"You speak as if you do not wish to live!" shouted the captain's son. "You stole precious satin from my house and stole my bride from me, but how shameless and brazen you remain!"

"It is you who are the thieves," answered the young woman. "It is you and your father who stole what is mine."

"Then I shall kill you and your father and mother! My men have already surrounded your house!"

"My father and mother have long fled," she quietly replied. "They've seen that the wrap I was found in has disappeared with me. They know your intent to harm my family and have long disappeared from this cursed land. They are safe."

"Fools!" The captain's son stomped his foot. "I'll kill you!"

He raised his sword and was about to bring it down on her neck.

The sky darkened. The captain's son froze, his arms still holding his sword aloft, and he looked up. Everyone looked up. Only the young woman stayed as she was.

It rained birds. The birds covered the courtyard and house, pecking and scratching whatever they could touch. Dishes broke, tables collapsed, food scattered, and utensils became covered in droppings. The captain and his wife, their relatives and guests, the servants who were carrying food back and forth, all screamed and scattered, as did the villagers who had gathered at the gate in wait for the fete to begin.

The captain's son frantically swung his sword in the air. He nicked the leg of a bird, and instead of blood, thread began to pour out of the wound. The blue and green thread whipped around his sword, his arm, and soon his whole body, squeezing his neck and chest, suffocating him to death.

The birds disappeared as abruptly as they'd appeared. The frightened servants ran about the rooms, calling for the captain and his wife. They found the captain wrapped in thread, his head and limbs separated from his torso. The captain's wife was also found strangled, her fingers gripping the thread around her neck, her eyes bulging and her tongue hanging from her mouth.

That's when the servants remembered the young woman who had embroidered the bird on the handkerchief. But it was too late, for they could not find her.

The wedding turned into a funeral. The relatives were left to carry out a different set of rituals than the ones they had anticipated. After they had gathered the bodies and body parts of the captain's family, they were discussing how they were to hold their funeral and to tell the bride-to-be's family what happened when someone shouted, "Fire!"

Everyone ran out of the house. A fire blazed from the storehouse and, like a bough bursting into blossoms in the spring, the house turned incandescent as well. The fire consumed the walls, the pillars, and the compound, and before the relatives and servants could bring any water, everything was on fire. Soon, the once looming house had turned to a pile of ash, and not a trace could be found of the bodies of the captain, his wife, or his son.

According to the legend of the village, on the night of the fire, a giant blue bird flew down and sat in front of the captain's house and laughed. At first light, the bird flew toward the river. And no one knew what became of the young seamstress and the pauper couple who raised her.

"That was the story," I told my sunbae. "A fun one, but I can't remember the title of the book. *The Memorabilia of the Three Kingdoms* or *The Historical Record of the Three Kingdoms* or something like that? But where the story came from, or during the era of which king, I remember none of that. But I remember most clearly the bird laughing at the end."

"It could be a book that escaped one of the labs," said my sunbae.

"A book can escape?" I laughed.

"It's a story about the handkerchief in Room 302," my sunbae said softly. "The bird embroidered on that handkerchief escapes sometimes. Why not a book?"

"You're joking, right? You're pulling one over on me?"

My sunbae smiled. And she said nothing more.

I never did see that book ever again. Maybe it really had escaped from one of the labs. I sometimes hear the flutter of wings and what sounds like a human voice from Room 302. I have no intention whatsoever of opening the door to look.

Why Does the Cat

"The cat in Room 206 is out today," said my sunbae.

"I'm sorry . . . it doesn't leave the Institute building, so it'll be all right," I said. Cats will do whatever they want and there's nothing anyone can do about it, but since I was the one who brought in the cat, I felt responsible.

"It's quite a clever animal," my sunbae mused. "It always meows before approaching me, letting me know it's there. It must know I can't see."

"It probably does!" I was pleased.

I am on my rounds.

I go down a floor and look intently around. On the landing of the stairwell, the cat looks up at me with its green eyes.

"I'm about to begin my shift," I explain. "Come with me?"

The cat gets up and walks to my side. I pat it on the head.

We go on my rounds together.

—Did you know that this house is haunted? I guess many don't realize it. Want me to tell you the story? It all began quite a long time ago.

It was an old house at the end of an alley.

The gate still looked sound, but over the wall, the garden has become overgrown, with some plants taller than people. On the door are countless yellowing and curling notification stickers from the post office about registered mail, and the windows of the house are broken or so filthy that it's hard to tell the glass panes apart from the walls.

It doesn't even have the usual gloominess or spookiness of an ordinary abandoned house—it's just decrepit and shabby. Explorers of haunted houses don't bother with it, not even kids on a dare.

There it stands, like a pile of trash at the end of a dead-end alley.

Just rotting there.

This house is where the man's last days had passed.

The man had an affair with his friend's wife. A very ordinary and common story.

He had known his friend since they were young and they were very close. They emceed each other's wedding receptions, and their parents and relatives all referred to the other as "your friend" and everyone understood who they meant.

Then the man's friend died. He hadn't been old, and it wasn't an accident but a disease. He had gone to the hospital because he didn't feel well, and it turned out there was nothing more that could be done. A situation out of a television drama, but also too ordinary and common. The man's friend thus left this world, and his wife, behind, and the man sobbed with his friend's parents in his arms as if he had lost a brother.

His visiting his friend's wife at first had been completely innocent. He was worried for his friend's wife, whom his friend had only just married and who now was left all alone in that house, forlorn and pale. She was cold and stiff at first, but once she understood the man was there to mourn his lifelong friend, they both cried together in genuine sadness and sorrow.

The man was aroused. The woman's tears, her loneliness, and her helpless, inconsolable suffering gave him something of a dark delight. Most men do not react this way to a woman crying, of course, and the man himself would never have admitted to it. He placated her, gave her a shoulder to cry on, shed tears with her, shared his memories with her, and as if it were the next thing on a list, took her to bed.

After their deed, the woman cried sorrowfully once again, and the man embraced the naked shoulders of his dead friend's widow, feeling an aching pleasure.

It was a deep satisfaction he had never known the likes of before.

The man had lost a friend, and the woman, her husband. They were the two main characters of a fateful, sad story, there was nothing they could do to turn back the hands of time, and therefore, anything was permitted to them to try to overcome this tragedy. Not that the man used such precise language to explain to himself why he did what he did, but such was the gist of it. He indulged in the usual self-justifications in the name of bringing succor to the vulnerable.

But time passes, wounds heal, and the human mind changes according to circumstances and environment. As the widow had no children and had lost her husband at a young age, she had no intention of remaining alone forever, nor the secret lover of her late spouse's friend, at that. Her family and friends, who knew nothing of this affair, also urged her not to mourn for too long and to find a new life for herself. Even her dead husband's family gave her their blessing and readied themselves for her to leave them for a new life.

The only person who didn't want to let her go was the man.

He liked to hold the widow against him and talk about his friend. He liked being reminded that those moments with his friend would never come again and then crying. There was only one person who understood him in those feelings, he felt, and that was the widow. They would reiterate that the only other person who shared this sadness was the other and would spend another night of desperate desire together.

It gave the man a rare and significant satisfaction. He did not want to give up this sense of himself as a tragic hero. Endlessly repetitive mourning, or any behavior that is endlessly repetitive, is generally not healthy, and professional help should be sought out when such behavior interferes with one's daily life. But the man had no intention of making healthy choices. Seeking psychological consultation is only possible if one wishes to leave unwell behaviors behind, but the man was very happy with how unwell he was, to the point of enjoying it. Which was why when the widow declared they should stop seeing each other, the man was at first devastated and then enraged.

As with many murders where the reason is stated to be "She refused to see me," the incident was considered compulsive and unpremeditated in a court of law or by law enforcement. The history of such compulsive and unpremeditated "She refused to see me" murders is long and varied, with recent examples including a man going to the house of the woman he considered his possession and threatening her with a weapon (April 2021), detonating a homemade bomb (October 2020), or killing the woman and all of her family (too many to cite).

So perhaps it was a little surprising how displeased the man was when the dead woman began to visit him. Logically, the man should've been happy that the woman he had so wanted to see, the one who had "refused" him to the point of putting him into a state of murderous rage, had seemingly changed her mind.

Instead, he was horrified.

The man was alone in the house.

The man's wife, because of her husband's frequent late nights and sleeping out and general neglect and coldness, had slowly grown more and more hurt, and when she had caught him sneaking in one dawn in clothes she'd never seen before, making nonsense excuses to her before exploding in anger at her, she had packed her bags and gone back to her mother's home. If the man's wife had never come back, that would have been the best choice she ever could have made in her life. But that comes later.

Anyway, at this point, the man was left alone at home and had fallen asleep drunk and woken in the middle of the night. His eyes had simply fluttered open.

The man got up and went to the living room. He saw the dead woman standing in the middle of it.

She just stood there and did nothing.

The man screamed. He turned on the light. The woman was gone. The living room was empty.

The man called his wife. She answered, irritated, asking him if he knew what time it was, and he begged her, saying he had done wrong, to come back, that he would do better, anything and everything he thought she might want to hear. The wife, having no idea her husband had murdered someone—nor that the victim of this murder had come to see him, just as he had so very much wanted, albeit when she'd been alive at least—accepted this fervent and rambling apology.

She came back. She shouldn't have.

The next night, his eyes opened once more. His wife slept soundly next to him. His phone showed the same time as the night before. The man got up carefully so as to not disturb his wife. He didn't want to get up, but he also wanted to shake off that dreadful feeling of terror.

He came out into the living room. The dead woman stood there once more.

All she did was stand and look toward his direction. The man turned on the living room lights. The dead woman disappeared.

The man came back to the bedroom and lay down next to his wife.

He didn't fall asleep for a long time.

The next night, and the night after that, his eyes opened in the middle of the night. And he crept into the living room, careful not to disturb his sleeping wife. When he saw the dead woman, he closed his eyes and turned on the living room light. He had tried turning on the light without looking at her, but he could not. Before he could see the light switch, he always met eyes with the woman's dark and empty gaze first. But the woman would disappear with the light, and the man could go back to bed and stare at the ceiling. The woman's gaze was always darker than the house was when he woke up at that mysterious hour. Every time he thought of her face, the man felt an inexplicable dread piercing his heart.

But he knew not where such dread came from and would eventually fall asleep in exhaustion.

His wife said one day, "I had an odd dream . . . There was a woman standing in our living room."

The man grew tense. "What woman?"

"I didn't know her," his wife murmured, dropping sugar into her coffee. "Her face was in shadow, but she was definitely standing in our living room. So I asked her who she was and why she was standing there."

She took a sip. The man waited. She took another sip.

"And then?" the man urged, trying not to sound strangled.

The woman stared into her coffee cup.

"What did the woman say?" the man asked again.

"I don't know. She didn't answer."

"It's just a dream," the man said. "It doesn't mean anything. Just forget it."

The woman kept staring into her cup. "But I keep having it. This dream. And . . ." She stopped. She took a long sip.

"And what?" His voice definitely sounded strangled.

"The woman is coming closer." She would not meet his eye. "I keep dreaming the same dream, but every time, the woman keeps getting closer to the bedroom."

"What?" The man stopped all pretense of eating his breakfast.

His wife lifted her coffee mug again. She lifted her worried gaze to her husband.

"What happens if she enters the bedroom?" she asked. And then, "There must be something in this house . . ."

As the man forced his hand to bring food up to his mouth and stuff it inside, he finally realized the reason for his nightly anxiety. More than the fact that he had killed the woman or that a dead woman kept coming to see him, the woman was also getting closer and closer to his bedroom.

He had to do something about this.

He went to the woman's house.

It was as he had left it. The foyer was clean, and the mailbox wasn't bursting.

When he entered and turned on the light, he was surprised the house was neat and looked lived-in, as if the woman had just stepped outside a moment ago.

She lay there on the bed, which was where he had killed her. Her dead skin had not decayed and was still soft and pale, her hair was still dark and lustrous, and her dead eyes, as they had in the man's hallucination, stared darkly. It felt as if she would sit up if he called her name. Only the red handprints on her neck attested to her death.

And next to her lay her cat, staring up at him with its green eyes.

"Hey," said the man to the cat, almost glad to see it. He said in a loud voice, "Why are you in here? You're not allowed on the bed."

The woman had owned the cat since before her marriage. She had loved this cat and had taken good care of it. The man neither liked nor hated this animal. When his friend was alive and the man would visit, he sometimes stroked the cat or played with it. But after his friend died and the widow tried to move on from mourning and their affair, it irked him that the woman cared so much for the cat. He did not want to let on that he felt jealous, and so he pretended to like the cat when she was watching.

He looked at the cat now. The cat also looked at him.

Slowly, so as to not scare the cat into moving or running out of the room, he backed away and closed the door, keeping their gazes locked the whole time.

When he turned around, there stood the woman.

He had never seen her face so up close before. He could not move. He could not make a sound. The woman's dark gaze froze him into place.

She opened her mouth.

— ...*not*...

The man couldn't answer. He could only stand and watch her red mouth and dark eyes as she formed the words.

—*. . . Do not . . .*

Her face came even closer to his.

—*Do not go . . .*

Her voice was a whisper now.

—*Die with me . . .*

Her cold breath brushed past the man's neck. The man closed his eyes.

He felt something soft against his ankle. It was warm and cushiony and slinked past his right foot, stepped on it, and went over to his left. The man looked down. The dead woman's cat stared up at him with its green eyes.

The man looked to the side. The dead woman was gone. There was only the late afternoon light weakly filtering into the empty living room.

The man ran out of there. He opened the door only a crack so the cat could not escape, looking down as he did so to make sure, and did not forget to close the door behind him.

There was much advice on the Internet about exorcisms and amulets and spells, but they all looked useless. The man could not afford to fail. He absolutely had to succeed on the first try.

The dead woman wasn't coming to the man's house so much as coming for the man himself. He needed to prevent her from finding him. Why she still hadn't been found was a mystery, but he had to prevent her from coming out until her body was discovered.

On a sleepless night, he had searched the Internet with bloodshot eyes and found what sounded like might do the trick.

Take an item the departed considered precious and use a nail or a stake to fix it in place.

There were some more words about blood or salt or red beans or talismans and such, but the man ignored them. This ought to be enough to be effective.

So one late evening, the man returned to the house of the dead woman. The man sat in the living room with the green-eyed cat in his arms as he awaited the hour he decided he would do it. When the hour came, he killed the cat by striking its head with a hammer and nailed the body of the cat against the headboard of the bed where the dead woman lay. The dead woman didn't move, and as always, she was a pale figure, with only his handprints a dark maroon on her neck. As he was about to close the door behind him, he thought he saw her turn her head to look at him when she hadn't.

He didn't think any more of it and left the house.

The dead woman was not waiting for him in the

living room. The man, as an experiment, turned off the lights, closed his eyes and counted to three, and opened them again. The woman did not reappear.

This satisfied him. He washed his hands in the bathroom sink, washed the hammer of the cat's blood, and as he did before, carefully closed the front door behind him and left the woman's house. He never went back.

The dead woman did not appear in his living room anymore.

The man's wife became pregnant. His life became a happy one.

The woman's decaying body was finally found in his dead friend's house, and the cat nailed to the wall made the authorities suspect some sort of revenge killing, which meant the police came to the man to question him.

But they were unable to pin anything on him, so that was it. Time passed, the case remained open, and the man could easily put the past behind him as he went on with his life.

His child ended up being a boy who looked very much like him. He was larger than average when he was born but began to talk and walk at the normal pace of normal babies. The sight of the baby's talking and walking made the man's wife suggest they have another child, and the man promised they would if he found a better job or got a raise, and their lives managed to settle down a little more. This was a sincere promise, and the man, even with his most conservative calculations, believed such a life was within his grasp.

The child experienced every normal thing a child experiences while growing up. He got sick from time to time, was mischievous and threw the occasional tantrum, and grew into a healthy boy who gave his parents both happiness and strife.

And the more he grew, the more a red birthmark on his neck became larger and clearer. The man had thought it was a bug bite at first and didn't think too much about it, but its presence bothered his wife to no end. The birthmark did not swell, and their child did not scratch at it, so it couldn't be a bug bite. At least, that's what the man said when the mother happened to be holding the child and looking at the blemish.

The wife took their son to the hospital the next day. The doctor took a close look and said it would probably go away as the child grew older. When the anxious mother asked several times what to do if it didn't go away, the doctor said something along the lines of it being fine because the child was a boy, and who cared if a boy had a birthmark or two? He added that she should still bring him in if the birthmark swelled or hardened or gave the child pain.

As his wife reported back what the doctor had said about the red birthmark, the man scoffed and said he had always known it was nothing.

Then the child said, "Cat."

"You want a cat?" The man laughed. "Your mother won't like it when it sheds."

"Cat," the child insisted once more.

"You like cats?" His tone turned more serious. "Shall we ask your mother about getting a cat?"

The boy shook his head. "Cat."

"So you don't want us to tell her?"

The boy looked up at him. "Why did you kill the cat?" he asked. "The cat didn't do anything to you."

The man looked down at him silently. The wide-eyed, limpid gaze of his child stared back at him, as if silently urging him to answer.

The man did not, and he stepped back.

His wife called for him and his child. The child smiled and ran to his mother.

The man stood where he was. He remembered the feel of the cat when it rubbed against his ankles.

—*Don't go.*

The voice of the dead woman whom he thought he'd silenced forever crept out of a corner of his mind.

—*Be dead with me...*

His wife found him shaking in place, unable to move.

The dead woman was back—which meant he needed to make a decision.

But the choices were not so clear to him this time.

He decided he would have to visit the dead woman's grave. He would drive a stake into her body, which would prevent the woman from haunting his child and stop her from coming after him. At least, that's what he believed would do the trick.

It had been a while since he visited his friend's grave. The dead woman, however, was not buried there with him. There was a mound and his friend's gravestone, but no trace of another burial.

He called his friend's parents. They were glad to hear from him at first, but then disconcerted when he asked about the grave of their late son's widow. Apparently, the dead woman's family had been adamantly against burying their daughter in her late husband's grave. They had berated her late husband's parents, that while there was nothing to be done about their son-in-law dying young, their perfectly healthy daughter had been murdered and the killer never found, for which they placed some blame on the family their daughter had married into. The man's friend's parents had understood this rage to be an expression of their grief and did not object when the dead woman's parents insisted on taking possession of her remains. They did not invite their former in-laws to her funeral, and therefore the man's friend's parents did not know where the dead woman's grave was. When the man begged them to call their former in-laws and ask, they replied that was too much to ask and hung up on him. They refused to pick up after that.

Having lost his most reliable source of information, he moved on to mutual acquaintances who might know, who all found his question very odd and off-putting and didn't answer him.

Then he called a former classmate whom he hadn't been close with, and when that classmate asked him if he had had some kind of relationship with the dead woman, the man quickly ended the call. The statute of limitations on his deed hadn't run out yet, after all.

He gave up looking for the dead woman's grave.

Not long after that, his son died. It was ruled an accident.

The man's wife fell into despair. She became

convinced her husband was responsible for their son's death and sued him. His wife's family paid for the lawsuit. The man denied it, but it was no use. The trial was messy and acrimonious, took a long time, and was very expensive. When it was over, the man had no wife, no house, no family, no life—nothing.

He hadn't intended to kill his son, not with any clarity, at least. The man wasn't so inhuman as to consciously kill his own son. But the man wasn't sure if the child's death was entirely accidental. It had happened in a split second. The man had simply not taken care of his son in that split second and turned his gaze away at a crucial moment. That's what it looked like from the outside.

The leading cause of accidental child death in the country was traffic accidents. His son was of the age where he was running around and not paying attention to possible dangers. There was a street crossing that almost everyone in the neighborhood jaywalked across. There were lights, but it was at the entrance of a small street that almost no one used except the people who lived on that street when they went to work or came back. The cars also had to make a right turn to enter, so they slowed down as they approached. Since there were hardly any cars and the ones that were there tended to slow down anyway, most people just crossed the street even when there was a red light. The teenagers watched the adults do it, and the children watched the teenagers do it. The man and his wife had to stop their child multiple times from running into the street at a red light.

And then came the moment when the man had to grab his child but turned his head and looked elsewhere instead. He saw a taxi coming in from the left and expected it to slow down before turning right. Or perhaps he had only wanted to believe it would slow down. The man could barely tell the difference at this point.

The child ran into the street, and the taxi driver did not slow down as he turned.

Throughout the funeral, as he listened to his wife's keening, the man kept wondering how the dead woman had managed to come back. Maybe the effectiveness of nailing down something the deceased loved was effective only for a short period of time. Maybe methods like that learned off the Internet were not so reliable after all. The man didn't know. There had been that night when his wife was working overtime and he was putting the child to bed when his son looked up at him, smiled, and then said, "Cat."

The man was startled. "There's no cat. All the cats have gone to bed now."

The boy was undaunted. He smiled again. "Cat."

"I said there is no cat!" the man said, annoyed.

"Why did you kill the cat, Dad?"

The man, bent over his son's bed, froze. He could do nothing but stare into his child's serious face.

"The cat didn't do anything to you," the boy murmured. He yawned. "Goodnight, Dad." He turned to his side.

The clear red birthmark on his pale neck came into the man's eye.

He remembered the dead woman's body lying on the bed: her skin, that had remained the same even after having died weeks ago; her black, lustrous hair; and the mark of the red handprints on her neck that was the only thing testifying to her death. He remembered that sight in the bedroom as if it were yesterday.

Maybe it wasn't a coincidence that he had searched on the Internet, before, of what were the leading causes of accidental deaths for children. The man did prioritize his own dread and fear above his wife and even the child of his own bloodline. It is a sad truth that there are many parents who remain of such a persuasion long after the birth of their children, whether they end up actually killing their children or not. Society, and the world at large, ought to be more aware that such selfish and egocentric attitudes are probably closer to true human nature than the oft-romanticized and mythologized unconditional and infinite love that we attribute to parent-child relationships.

At any rate, the dead child could say nothing now, and the man, long after the child's funeral and the departure of his wife, would continue to get up in the middle of the night to repeatedly turn the living room light off and on again.

The dead woman did not reappear. This only made the man more nervous and afraid. He called around again demanding to know where the dead woman was buried. This resulted in most of his friends and acquaintances cutting him off for good. The rest cut him off after he was arrested at a cemetery where he had been digging through a grave using a long metal stake.

One long and dark night, the man turned on all the lights in his apartment and left it behind him forever.

—*Wait for it. Here it comes.*

The moon disappears. Darkness unfurls over the alley. The streetlights are long ago smashed and covered in cobwebs.

A shadow appears in the dirty and smashed windows. It moves. Then suddenly, the lights of the crumbling house switch on. The shadow becomes two, then three, then seems to become two again.

The man has become trapped in his fear and suffering, it ties him to this house, the last one he had lived in after leaving his old life. He cannot escape it. This is how foolish people can be, trying to hold on to a moment, a finite amount of time. The man had wanted to hold on to the woman inside their shared grief forever, so in a sense, the man's wish has come true. The dead man, in fear of the dead woman, still turns on the lights every night. Two shadows appear behind the dirty glass of the window. The moment the shadows move, the light goes off. The dead man turns the lights on again. Through the broken panes, the shadow of a head flits by. The lights go off again. The dead man turns them on. Two shadows appear, and one of them approaches the other. The moment the two shadows meet, the light turns off again.

—*The woman left a long time ago.*

I stare at the house that had swallowed the man's body and the shadows inside it. The dead man's guilt turns the lights off and brings forth the shadow of the dead woman, who is long gone. The dead man's fear rejects the darkness and turns on the lights of the house again. The dead man's guilt brings forth the shadow of the dead child, and the dead man's fear once again turns off the lights. This is all that is left to the dead man. Guilt, and fear. The lights switch on. The lights switch off.

—But why did he have to kill me?

The cat with the green eyes and the nail in its neck stares up at me as it asks this.

—When he didn't really hate me, and I didn't do anything to him.

I couldn't find the right way to explain to a cat how a human might be foolish enough to resort to violent methods to rid themselves of a shadow of their own making, so I asked it a question instead.

"Shall I take out the nail in your neck?"

—It doesn't hurt me anymore.

The cat then rubbed itself in a figure eight around my ankles as cats do. Its fur, in death, is cold and lustrous and silky, and it breaks my heart. The man hadn't known the cat would return to haunt him.

—Humans are not good at knowing, in general.

What we can see and hear and touch in this world is very limited. And so perhaps it's true we don't know much about the world at all. We like to say there's nothing new under the sun, but we don't have the slightest inkling of how many things there are, indeed, under the sun.

"Want to come with me?" I said, bending over and stroking the green-eyed cat. "I know a place you can be safe in."

The cat licks my finger in answer. Its tongue is soft

and rough at the same time. I pat its cold, silky head, and wait for the sun to rise. Hoping that I can bring a little bit of consolation to those who are most vulnerable, be they shadows under the sun.

Sunning Day

One day out of the month, I go to work during daylight hours.

It's called Sunning Day. We bring out the things stored in the Institute and expose them, on the lawn, to sunlight and wind. My sunbae explained that this was necessary for the expedited freeing of those that haunt the objects. We all wear safety goggles and masks and gloves and the researchers go around with electronic equipment, verifying the serial number and registration information of each item and updating them with pictures, which they use to see if there are any changes, and if there are none, how long has it been since the last change. The sight of all these mismatched objects lying out on the lawn makes me think we run a lost and found center. I wonder what item I might leave behind someday.

"Don't think of what you'll leave behind. Just leave. That's the best way."

My sunbae sounds adamant about this. I agree with her. But that's easier said than done. Otherwise, the Institute wouldn't have ended up with so many items—it wouldn't exist at all.

We don't take out everything, of course. The handkerchief with the embroidered bird and flowers on the bough stays in Room 302. If the bird gets angry or the branch and flowers smell moldy, the researchers, after taking specific precautions, puts it out under the moonlight. Apparently, before they knew to do such a thing, the handkerchief's red and yellow flowers had caught fire and the blue-and-green bird had flown all the way to the horizon, laughing uproariously like a human all the way. Who knew where it had been trying to fly to. The burning flowers were too hot for bare hands, and the bird turned large and threatening, its wings covering half the sky and its beak a lethal weapon. The researcher in charge of it blocked the sun from the handkerchief with a bit of waterproof foil they had been using to lay the objects on, and that helped shrink the fire and the bird. They wrapped the handkerchief in the foil and carefully moved it back into the Institute building. Ever since then, they never put out the handkerchief under the sunlight.

The deputy director says this is what happens to objects that have been haunted for too long.

"Like overstaying their rental contract?" I don't know why I said that, but at least the deputy director laughs.

"Right? I wonder what could possibly be the deposit that blue bird wants to get back, if it's still here way past its move-out date."

"I suppose the researchers will figure it out," I muse.

The deputy director agrees.

It turns out that the fluttering and squawking I heard on my rounds once were not from the ancient blue bird in Room 302 but a seagull in Room 103. I learn this only when the researcher in charge of it brings it out for sunning. The researcher explains to me that a taxidermist had stuffed a seagull for no other reason than wanting it for his living room, but at night, he would hear fluttering. This was soon accompanied by squawking and attacks upon the fridge and garbage. But it was really brought here to the Institute when it began to make a mess of droppings on the other taxidermized animals and the floor. A very seagull-like revenge. If I had a perfectly normal life of flying around and then was made into a stuffed and still animal model all of a sudden, I would mourn my hardened wings every night as well.

I don't think the researcher in charge of the seagull enjoyed cleaning its droppings every morning, but thankfully, the seagull seems to have finally moved on. This is its last sunning, the researcher explains, a precautionary sunning, if you will. Under the bright and hot midday sun, the seagull looks exhausted, and its glass eyes, lifeless. The researcher lights a stick of ceremonial incense in front of it. Once the sun sets, it will be carefully wrapped and moved into the Institute's storage facility. A new object will be brought into Room 103, where it will be taken care of until what haunts it is ready to move on.

My cat, as well, will move on eventually. The deputy director had warned me after I had brought it into the Institute that if I keep opening the door for it during my rounds, it will be more hesitant to move on. She scolded me on the ethics of a human keeping a cat tethered to this world when it was a human who had given it so much pain and suffering in life. Her admonishment did have me imagining the brown fur of the cat enlarging to cover the sky as its green eyes catch fire and giant paws coming down to swipe at us all. Cats are always ready to leave, and if a researcher attempted to use that waterproof foil on them, they'd slip right out of it like they're made of liquid. The cat is already turning more and more transparent and slips through my fingers like water. Only the giant nail in its neck grows colder and harder, in an ominous way. Once the cat is gone, this hideous murder weapon will be brought out once a month to the Institute lawn for sunning. I don't like to think about that too much.

But for now, the cat is enjoying the warmth of the sun. Next to it is the deputy director's sheep. All the animals of the Institute seem to get along, in general. On sunning days, the cat likes to groom the sheep, and sometimes crawls up on its wool and falls asleep. The sheep's wounds are also disappearing, and new wool is growing over its scars. When that live-streamer who infiltrated us for content stole the shoe, the sheep ended up with multiple new wounds and lost wool, according to the deputy director. Just as I worry over the cat, the deputy director worries over the sheep. Unlike with my cat, however, her sheep represents a whole flock, and it will take many sunning days for them all to move on.

Sunning days aren't always mild and pleasant, either. We must always be careful of objects made of iron, or any sharp object. I once glimpsed a glitter of a sunning object from afar—only for just a moment—and ended up with wounds on my face and neck. Nothing too serious, but it was scary to see my own blood.

I sometimes encounter objects I had never heard of before, on sunning days. Today, it's something the researchers have created a wide space for, with several of them straining hard to carry it out into the sun—practically dragging it on the ground more than carrying it. A black sports coat. Seemingly ordinary, but there is nothing ordinary about anything in this institute, of course. The researchers take care to lay it flat on the ground, so it receives as much sun as possible.

The jacket starts to smoke. Its acrid smell burns my throat, and I can't breathe. My sunbae grabs my arm and draws me back. "Best not to stand too close to that," she murmurs. "I think something is about to come out of it."

"What something?" I ask, unintelligently.

My sunbae doesn't answer. She raises her face to the sky and takes a few sniffs of the unbearable, threatening smoke and turns her head.

"Northwesterly," she notes out loud.

And the jacket starts to jerk. All the researchers step back.

"The jacket is moving," I whisper. My sunbae does not let go of my arm as she also moves backward.

Something that looks like glass marbles roll out of the jacket. They sparkle in the sun and are beautiful, clearly magical. I want to pick one up. But as I step forward, my sunbae squeezes my arm, stopping me.

The marbles keep rolling out. They fill the wide space the researchers made for them and start to smoke like the jacket had. The air is full of that acrid, sticky, dreadful smell now. I could understand why the researchers wore masks and gloves. I wish I'd brought them myself.

The jacket keeps letting out marbles, and the sparkling spheres hiss and smoke and dissipate in the lawn of the Institute. When no more marbles emerge from the jacket and they have all vanished in the sun, the researchers take photos and sprinkle salt all over the places the marbles had been.

"Is it over?" I ask.

"Wait a bit more," said my sunbae. "If it's over, the researchers will tell us."

And that's when the jacket begins to move again. The researchers, who'd been sprinkling salt, leap back.

Glass shards erupt from the jacket, and a researcher who had been standing too close shrieks and jumps away.

I'm so surprised that I'm about to bolt when my sunbae grabs my sleeve and turns me around to face the other direction.

"It's northwest of us," she explains. "It can't come in the direction of the sun."

I do as she tells me to and stare toward the sun. I feel little shards hit my back and the nape of my neck. But unlike the flash of light from a blade that hit me on another sunning day, the glass shards do not pierce my skin or even my clothes. I look back. The glass shards melt away when they touch humans, it seems. The researchers are calmly turning the jacket so it receives the sunlight better. It doesn't seem nearly as heavy as when they had first brought it out.

The cat, which had been hiding behind the sheep, pokes out its head. It goes up to a glass shard in front of the sheep and bats it. The shard doesn't melt.

"Don't touch that," I say to the cat. My sunbae is still grabbing ahold of my arm. "Sunbae, I have to pick that up before it harms anyone."

"Don't touch that," my sunbae says, echoing what I said to the cat.

I go up to the cat and sheep. The sheep's wool has glasslike slivers in it as well. It is otherwise calm and just stares blankly at me. The cat still bats the shard. I have no gloves, so I draw my sleeve over my hand. First, I gently knock off the transparent fragments in the sheep's wool. The second my sleeve touches them, the slivers melt away like ice splinters.

The cat seems disappointed when I melt away the shard it played with as well.

"I'm sorry. But it's not good for you."

I stroke the cat's head, and it lets itself be stroked as if to forgive me for taking away its plaything. Just as the shard had melted away at my touch, the cat's head also, sadly, is becoming faint and less substantial under my hand.

Sunning day is coming to an end. The jacket, having released its marbles and shards of unresolved hate and injustice, is now as light as an ordinary jacket. The researchers surround it as they take photographs and note down on their devices what happened.

"It seems to have been from an accident," my sunbae says after the researchers carefully folded the jacket and took it back inside. "The wearer tried to flee during a fire but couldn't find the exit, so they jumped."

"You can see that?" I marvel.

My sunbae scoffs. "I can't see anything, much less that. You just get a feeling for these things, once you work here long enough."

I'm a bit embarrassed. But still more curious.

"What was all that about the northwest? Why can't they come toward the sun?"

"They say that the undead move in a northwesterly direction," my sunbae explains. "If you feel the airflow suddenly change, it's best to head southeast, or if you're not sure where that is, any direction where there's light."

The sun is setting. We salt down every corner of the Institute lawn. The deputy director lights some incense as an offering.

We return to the work of protecting the undead from the terrors of our daylight world.

Afterword: On the Joys of Ghost Stories

I often get asked about what to do in a writer's block situation. The first thing to do is to think about why you're blocked. If it's a matter of not knowing enough about your topic or material, you just have to do some research. If you're tired or hungry or sick, eat something or drink some water (it's so important to stay hydrated), or go to the hospital or pharmacy, and rest.

If, despite resting and eating and drinking and researching you are *still* blocked, a good method of overcoming this is to write a ghost story.

I love ghost stories. A lot. I love hearing them, reading them, and writing them. Once I start thinking about at which point the appearance of the ghost would prove the scariest, the writing starts to flow again.

Midnight Timetable was not a deadline or a chore for me but a really fun amusement park of a book to work on. To write an entire book of ghost stories! I had so much fun doing it.

YOU CAN'T COME IN HERE

Because I love ghost stories so much, I'm always on the lookout for urban legends on the Internet or television programs that specialize in them, and I've noticed that social media has made the exploration of haunted houses something of a popular hobby these days.

I beg you not to indulge. "You Can't Come in Here" and "Cursed Sheep" were both written with this request in mind.

The Institute in this book does not exist, but there are plenty of abandoned hospitals, factories, and houses. You may not find any ghosts there, but it's too easy to get into an accident and injure yourself. Buildings that are abandoned are just that, abandoned, and no one is taking care of their safety, often for years or decades. You might get exposed to toxins or diseases at abandoned factories or hospitals. And also, while abandoned buildings may look like no one cares about them, they probably fall under someone's ownership and laws against trespassing would apply.

It would also be a huge inconvenience for the people who live around the building if people kept going in and out of it at night and making a fuss.

You can't come in here. I repeat, you can't come in here.

TUNNEL

I'm bad at driving and scared of driving at night. I once did a book event in Gyeonggi Province where I suddenly found myself on a dark mountain road where I could see nothing around me except the yellow median painted in the middle of the road, and I drove for a long time just shaking in fear. At the book event, I mentioned this and said it might be fun to write a ghost story where all you could see was an endless yellow median, and the audience cheered the idea. So I wrote it. That was a fun event, and the bookstore itself was very cozy and pretty. I just happen to be terrible at night driving.

Tunnels are the same. To get from Pohang, which is where I live, to anywhere in Korea, I inevitably have to go through a series of tunnels. Because I've driven through many tunnels at night, I became quite determined to write a ghost story set in a tunnel as well.

But when I was writing this one, there happened to be a real accident and fire that occurred in a tunnel resulting in many casualties, and because I drive through so many tunnels I was terrified by this news as it could easily happen to me at any time.

My thoughts are with the victims, and I hope for the full recovery of those injured. I also hope more safeguards will be put in place so there are no more tunnel accidents.

THE BLUE BIRD AND THE HANDKERCHIEF

The first part of "The Handkerchief" is based on a true story involving the family of a friend of mine whose mother passed away. My parents' generation, who were born right before the outbreak of the Korean War and thus had to survive a difficult time, seem to very commonly think that pitting their children against each other is the best way to raise children who are loyal to you. But physical abuse or forced starvation are not the only kinds of parental abuse. Favoritism and discrimination can hurt all siblings deeply, and such wounds come back to haunt you even decades later in unpredictable ways. Although maybe not as unpredictable a way as a haunted handkerchief.

Speaking of handkerchiefs, I needed to figure out where such a handkerchief might come from so I read through the *Memorabilia of the Three Kingdoms* and the *Historical Records of the Three Kingdoms* on the Database of Korean History maintained by the

National Institute of Korean History. That's where I learned that when the Gaya confederacy fell, their people became what we would now call refugees and suffered all sorts of difficulties and discrimination at the hands of the Silla people. I read one particular story of a Kaya family whose patriarch was murdered and his wife and son were placed in the home of a high Silla official where the official attempted to rape the woman and ended up killing her while her son fled and returned later on to exact revenge. The record was short and impactful and, unlike many of the other narratives in the *Memorabilia*, was a scary story with a clear beginning, middle, and end. But later on, when I checked back in the process of writing this novel, I could not find it on the database to save my life. Which is somehow very much appropriate for this book.

Kaya became extinct in the sixth century. I read about the displaced people of Kaya in the twenty-first century. Perhaps it's the cries and sorrow of the vulnerable that echo ever more deeply and strongly through time.

GHOST GRUDGE

A very popular ghost in Korean ghost stories is, of course, the "virgin ghost," the wronged young woman who has a grudge against someone living. How Koreans became a nation of grudges is excellently explored further in Jeon Heyjin's *Women Who Become Ghosts*. But I've always felt sorry for any ghost who holds a grudge and is condemned to float around the world of the living. I will always hope that the perpetrator would meet their downfall by their own evil ways and that their victims find peace somehow.

So my preoccupation as a Korean used to these ghost stories that center around such han was to not conclude with some educational moral at the end. Writing a scary story in full-length novel form is harder than it may seem, because the reason a horror story or an urban legend is frightening is because it handles a world that we can't completely comprehend. The more you write about something you cannot completely comprehend, the clearer it becomes that it is a thing that is unknowable and that gets boring. So when we attempt to write a long ghost story, we usually either have to make it into a mystery, to find out how that ghost became a ghost, or a thriller, where the main character tries to stop some terrible thing from happening once again. I wanted to avoid both forms—I wanted to write a real ghost story, not a mystery or a thriller masquerading as one. And that's how I came up with this form of interconnected short stories. I hope each story felt like visiting a different lab room in the Institute.

MIDNIGHT TIMETABLE

I moved to Pohang in 2021, when the pandemic still raged. Pohang Bus Terminal has a separate ticket window for night buses. Since it's a port city, Pohang has always had an influx of foreigners, which means the bus terminal has many signs in English. The night bus schedule that hangs over the night bus ticket window, for example, helpfully has the English words MIDNIGHT TIMETABLE emblazoned on it. These two words in juxtaposition felt very poetic and mysterious to me, and I've always wanted to use them in a story.

And that's how this book came to be called *Midnight Timetable*.

Bora Chung is a writer and translator whose works include the National Book Award finalist and International Booker Prize–shortlisted *Cursed Bunny* and *Your Utopia*. She has an MA in Russian Studies from Yale University and a PhD in Slavic literature from Indiana University. She has taught Russian language and literature and science fiction at Yonsei University and translates modern literary works from Russian and Polish into Korean.

Anton Hur is the author of *Toward Eternity* and the translator of many iconic Korean SFF works including Bora Chung's *Cursed Bunny*, Kim Choyeop's *If We Cannot Go at the Speed of Light*, Lee Young-do's *The Bird That Drinks Tears*, Kim Sung-il's *Blood of the Old Kings*, and Park Seolyeon's *A Magical Girl Retires*.

RAISING READERS
Books Build Bright Futures

Thank you for reading this book and for being a reader of books in general. As an author, I am so grateful to share being part of a community of readers with you, and I hope you will join me in passing our love of books on to the next generation of readers.

Did you know that reading for enjoyment is the single biggest predictor of a child's future happiness and success?

More than family circumstances, parents' educational background, or income, reading impacts a child's future academic performance, emotional well-being, communication skills, economic security, ambition, and happiness.

Studies show that kids reading for enjoyment in the US is in rapid decline:

- In 2012, 53% of 9-year-olds read almost every day. Just 10 years later, in 2022, the number had fallen to 39%.
- In 2012, 27% of 13-year-olds read for fun daily. By 2023, that number was just 14%.

Together, we can commit to **Raising Readers** and change this trend. How?

- Read to children in your life daily.
- Model reading as a fun activity.
- Reduce screen time.
- Start a family, school, or community book club.
- Visit bookstores and libraries regularly.
- Listen to audiobooks.
- Read the book before you see the movie.
- Encourage your child to read aloud to a pet or stuffed animal.
- Give books as gifts.
- Donate books to families and communities in need.

Books build bright futures, and **Raising Readers** is our shared responsibility.

For more information, visit **JoinRaisingReaders.com**

Sources: National Endowment for the Arts, National Assessment of Educational Progress, WorldBookDay.org, Nielsen BookData's 2023 "Understanding the Children's Book Consumer"